Love Thy Sister, Guard Thy Man

by

Kimberlee R. Mendoza

The Russell Family Series

Love Thy Sister, Guard Thy Man

COPYRIGHT © 2016 by Kimberlee R. Mendoza

Cover Art by *Kim Mendoza*

The Wild Rose Press, Inc.
PO Box 708
Adams Basin, NY 14410-0708
Visit us at www.thewildrosepress.com

Publishing History
Second New Adult Edition, 2016
Print ISBN 978-1-5092-0959-0
Digital ISBN 978-1-5092-0956-9

The Russell Family Series
Published in the United States of America

"*Get* up." Cassi tugged on the comforter, then tried to yank Melena's pillow away. "I need to talk to you."

"I'm not in the mood." Melena repositioned her pillow. "Especially for you."

"Too bad. I want to know why you acted like such a wench last night."

"What? Sorry, I can't hear you."

Cassi yanked the pillow free and onto the floor. "What was your major deal last night?"

"Sorry, what was that?"

Cassi stomped over to the stereo and turned it off. "I said...why'd you act like such a jerk last night?"

Melena didn't want to answer. The anger she felt was sure to spill over and things would be said that shouldn't be. She faced the wall praying for patience.

Her sister stepped on the bed, climbed over her body, and wedged herself between the wall and Melena's stomach.

"You're on my arm. Get off!"

"Then talk to me."

"Fine, you want to know why I was angry." Melena pushed up on her elbows. "Because you stole two things from me in one night. What were you doing there anyway? It's not even your crowd."

"A girl from my school invited me." Cassi shrugged. "I don't know why you got all weepy about that bracelet. It wasn't even that cute."

Melena pushed back the thought of her birthday gift sinking in the sand. "Where did you meet Dylan?"

"At the party, why?" Her lips pinched tight. "Oh, I get it. You're jealous because I saw him first."

Praise for Kimberlee R. Mendoza

"Ms. Mendoza penned an edifying story with highly likeable characters. Natural dialogues, clever and witty conversations—things just seem to flow effortlessly. All you need to do is just go with the flow. I felt connected with the characters as I devoured the novel. It is definitely an easy-to-read treat and I am already looking out for more of her novels. I highly recommend this!"

~Tulip, Long & Short of It Reviews

~*~

"I finished reading this story with a smile on my face."

~Marlene, Fallen Angel Reviews (5 Angels)

~*~

"Thank you Ms. Mendoza for bringing us Melena and all the wonderful and very real characters of *LOVE THY SISTER, GUARD THY MAN.*"

~BrandyWine, Enchanting Reviews (5 Enchantments)

~*~

"It was incredibly engaging for a young adult novel."

~Michelle Sutton, author

Dedication

In loving memory of Grandma Coulson, Grandma June,
Grandpa Van, and Granny Ruiz…
~*~
Thank you all for believing in me.
The world is a better place because you were in it,
but it will never be the same now that you are gone.

Chapter One

Melena floated in his arms around the ballroom floor. Mist swirled around her ankles. He whispered in her ear. She asked him to repeat it, but the music grew louder and louder as he released her hand. The clash of a cymbal cut the room as he drifted farther from her.

She peeked out from under her pillow. *Bummer!* Her alarm clock blared an old 80s tune and read 7:00 a.m. She had to be in devotions in the chapel in less than thirty minutes. Groaning, she rolled toward the cabin window and lifted the shade. Early morning sunlight flooded the room. She squinted and turned away.

Her head was still foggy, but that didn't stop the butterflies from dancing in her stomach. Every time she thought about Dylan Hart, the phantom creatures increased their rhythm. *Ah!* She flopped on her back and stared at the wood ceiling. *Hopeless.* She couldn't block him from her mind. The guy sent electrical currents up her spine—six foot one, thin, muscular-build, shoulder-length blond hair, and hazel eyes. Hot? Oh, yeah. One hundred and one.

Her best friend, April, had talked her into spending a week of summer vacation at youth camp in the Cuyamaca Mountains above San Diego. Tonight was their final night. Melena wished she could get up the nerve to go talk to him. A deep breath, then she folded out of bed, ready for another day of admiring Dylan from afar.

****

"Just go over there and introduce yourself," April said.

Melena stopped her spoon of cornflakes mid-air. "What? Who?"

"You're kidding, right?" April pushed her cropped, blonde hair over her ear and leaned across the table on both elbows. "Only the guy you've been staring at since we got here. Dylan Hart."

"You're insane." Melena's cheeks heated. "I haven't been staring at anyone."

"Melena Harrison! How dare you lie to your best friend?"

Melena lifted the bowl to drain its contents but thought better of it when he glanced her way. Returning the bowl to the table, she dabbed her mouth with a napkin, then wiped the table, ignoring her friend's insistent stare.

"Oh, no." April slapped the table. "You're not going to play that innocent game with me. I know you too well."

Melena met April's eyes. "Okay, so I think he's cute. What's the big deal?"

"The big deal is you haven't once tried to go out with a guy—*ever*. You're biological clock is ticking."

Melena gasped, then pinched her lips together. "Please. I'm eighteen."

"So, my cousin Letty was married and with child by that age."

"*Hello*. Letty lives in Arkansas where fifteen is old." Melena placed her hands over her eyes and peeked through the cracks between her fingers. Dylan leaned against the far wall next to a guy named Chad. His friend was short and much stockier than Dylan with spiky black hair and a kind smile. She knew Chad because he played bass in her church worship band.

Dylan scanned the room, his shoulders back and his jaw firm—confident. A trait Melena wished she could purchase. It was so attractive.

"Earth to Melena." April waved her hand in front of Melena's face.

She blinked.

"Just go talk to him. You're killing me."

Melena scooted back in the plastic chair and reached for her tray. "Eighteen is not old."

"Come on, Mel. The short one is mine." April jumped up from the table and sauntered in their direction.

"His name's Chad." Melena caught her arm. "And you have a boyfriend."

"So, this isn't about me." April shook her arm free, smirked, and started for them again.

A queasy feeling swept through Melena's stomach. Trying to stop April, once she'd made up her mind, was like stopping a bear at a picnic. Lots of people looked at April's petite stature and assumed she was weak. But they'd be wrong. She was a spirited woman of fortitude. And right now, that determination was about hooking up her best friend. *Too bad I'm her best friend.*

"Mel, come here."

Melena glanced across the room. April stood within inches of her dream date. *No mercy, huh, April?*

She waved for Melena to join them.

Melena busied herself with picking up her trash,

taking her time to empty the tray, before finally walking the green mile. Head down, she studied the checkered tile. Afraid of what was sure to happen. *Absolute humiliation at my expense. This is so not cool.*

"Dylan. This is my friend, Melena."

He met her shy gaze, sending a prickly sensation through her body.

"Dylan just moved to Del Mar." She bobbed her head and smiled an annoying smile that only meant one thing—get in the game.

Melena cleared her throat. "Um…where did you move from?"

"Jacksonville, Florida. My mom is a marine biologist." He smiled, revealing a small dimple on the side of his cheek. She tried to stay focused. "She got a position at Scripps in La Jolla."

"They have cool tide pools." *Yeah, that just came out of my mouth. Cool tide pools. What am I? Twelve?*

Chad stepped forward with crossed arms and a sly grin. "So, do you girls have dates for the nature hike this evening?"

Melena's heart accelerated. She opened her mouth, but nothing came.

April elbowed her.

She found her breath, and the words tumbled out. "No, we don't."

Chad raised an eyebrow. "Hard to believe you two beautiful women don't have dates."

Okay, now he's just being corny.

Dylan smiled. "Well, hang with us. It'll be fun."

Melena smiled despite her stomach's desire to toss her cereal. She couldn't believe it. She had a date.

Chapter Two

Dylan stumbled to the cabin, panting. A strong smell of pine and eucalyptus drifted with the breeze. He closed his eyes and breathed.

A second later, Chad collapsed on the wooden steps, unscrewed the top of a water bottle, and poured it over his head.

"The air is too thin to be running." Dylan leaned against the log wall and rolled his shoulders forward. His muscles tightened in complaint.

Chad shook his wet head like a dog. "Dude, you're the one who had the brilliant idea to run before dinner. We should have gone swimming."

A cramp shot through Dylan's rib cage. He gripped his side and grunted. "Yeah, what was I thinking?" His T-shirt and shorts clung to his skin, sweat dripped down his face. "I need a shower."

Chad glanced at his watch, then used the railing to stand. "Dinner started ten minutes ago."

"I think I'll skip dinner and just get ready for the hike."

"Oh, right. You got yourself a date." Chad punched his arm and smiled. "Sweet."

Dylan shook his head. "We're going as a group."

"Nah, she's into you." Chad reached for a stick on the ground and tossed it into a group of trees. "She's been checking you out all week."

5

Dylan's heart skipped. He looked at the ladies' cabin just a few yards away. "Really?"

Chad clutched Dylan's shoulder and leaned to his ear. "You're not all that observant, huh?"

Not really, no. His ex-girlfriend had told him that before. Apparently, he didn't notice anything. It made him cringe when she used to say things like, "I got a new haircut and you didn't even notice." How could he? It always looked the same—pulled up into a ponytail. It was exhausting.

But he had learned a valuable lesson during their year-long romance. *If I care about someone, I have to make her a priority.* That's how he'd treat his next girl. Dylan nudged the cabin door open. "What do you know about her?"

Chad followed him in and walked to his bunk. "Not that much. Sometimes she goes to our youth group. Her dad used to be the college pastor at our church until he got divorced. Now I think he's on staff at some mission's organization."

"Hmm?" Dylan lifted his shirt over his head. "She seems cool. Maybe a little shy."

Chad climbed up on the second bunk and folded his legs. "I don't think she's ever had a boyfriend, or at least no one has ever talked about one. She's gorgeous, but blushes whenever a guy gets too close."

"Yeah, I noticed." He dug a clean shirt from his duffel bag and grabbed a towel. "See you in a bit."

****

Melena buttoned the waistband of her jeans and studied her fourth outfit in the mirror. Nothing seemed to fit her long, thin body right. Usually, shirts were too short or too big. Shopping had always been an issue.

Maybe that was why she shunned high fashion. It wasn't fun. She wrinkled her nose at the rose colored T-shirt. "Do I look okay? Maybe the green one was better."

April stopped combing her hair and turned from the mirror. Her eyes skimmed Melena from the floor up. "It's a nature walk, Mel."

"Yes, but I have date." She beamed.

"You've always looked great in pink. It compliments your lovely olive complexion." April batted her eyes.

"Okay, now you're just being obnoxious."

April tossed her hair with her hand. "It's a gift. Now finish up, or you'll miss your date."

Melena pulled on the white scrunchy and shook her strawberry-blonde hair upside down. She flipped her head back and smoothed it with a brush. The long layers were actually cooperating for once.

"You're beautiful. Ready?"

"Yeah, I guess." Melena snatched a denim coat from her bunk and met April at the door.

"Are you wearing that jacket?"

Melena stared at the jean material in her hand with wide eyes and flared nostrils. *Is it ugly?* "Yeah, why?"

"No, reason. Are you ready?"

"What's wrong with the jacket?"

"Nothing, Mel." She grinned. "It's warm, so I thought I'd ask."

"Fine then, let's go."

April popped a piece of bubble gum in her mouth and grabbed a flashlight. The two climbed the dirt trail to where the group had already begun to form at the top of the grassy knoll. A slight breeze moved but the air was still warm.

Sweat beaded in Melena's hand. *Am I nervous? Yeah, about this coat.* "April, wait. I don't think I want to take my jacket. It's hot. I'll end up lugging it the whole way."

"Are you sure? What if it gets cold later?"

"Yeah, I'm sure." She wasn't sure, just nervous. She ran back down the dirt trail, up the steps, and tossed the jacket on the nearest bunk. Her stomach cramped. She hadn't had a date since—well, since birth. It wasn't that she was *ugly*, just shy when it came to guys. The only reason she had one now was because April was persistent and Chad was forward.

Big breath in. She inhaled until it hurt. *Exhale.* Slowly, she breathed out through her lips. *I can do this. Right?* She ran back to the mirror and checked her makeup. "Probably not, but you're going to," she said to her reflection.

She hurried back up the path. The sun had begun to set behind the tall pines, casting vast shadows throughout the forest. Thousands of sparkling lights paraded in the cloudless sky. *Inhale. Exhale.*

The two guys waited at the top of the hill. The pain in her stomach tightened. Dylan looked incredible. He wore a black T-shirt, gray hoodie, and jeans. His hair was pushed behind his ears and a tiny mole above his lip accented his smile.

Pastor Scott hopped up on a rock, adjusted his glasses, and cleared his throat. "Okay, ladies and gentlemen. We're all adults, so I'll make this real simple. Stay close together, but not *too* close."

Everyone laughed.

"Stay on the trails and don't feed the animals."

"Sorry, Dylan. You'll have to starve," Chad said.

The group laughed again.

"Okay, I guess that is it. Let's move out." Pastor Scott jumped down, grabbed his clipboard, and started for the path between the trees.

Chirping crickets, hooting owls, and the occasional howling coyote set the music for the hike. A steady hum of chatter and the scuffing beat of feet added to the nightly orchestra. Swaying flashlights lined the dirt trail, casting an orange glow on the band of young adults. Melena hoped their loud approach would scare off any unwanted wildlife.

Chad and April fell back a few feet, debating Mac versus PC.

The group pulled ahead a bit. Panic pumped through Melena's veins at the realization she was now alone with *him*. *What should I say?* She had hoped they'd all walk together. She glanced over at Dylan. *Man, he's gorgeous.*

He met her gaze.

She looked away.

They walked in silence for a while and she began to wonder if maybe he was shy, too. *Are we going to do this the whole way?* She sighed.

His voice cut through the silence. "In Florida, I had a potbellied pig."

She giggled. "Really? As a pet?"

"Yeah, he was a runt on my uncle's farm. We saved him just before the ax was to fall."

"That's cute. Like Wilber."

"Hey, that's his name."

"Really?" Melena smiled. "All I've ever had was a goldfish. I want a cat, but with my home situation, it

9

isn't likely."

He glanced at her sideways. "Home situation?"

Why did I say that? She didn't want to get into all her baggage. *Well, at least we're talking.* "Um...my folks are divorced. I float from one to the other."

He raised an eyebrow. "Hmm? Really? Even now that you're older?"

"It's complicated." She waved and shook it off. The bushes moved next to her. She jumped against him.

Dylan laughed. "Probably just a bird or something."

"It's the *or something* I'm worried about."

He studied her. "I bet you're a city girl through and through, huh?"

She flipped her hair over her shoulder and smiled. "What gave it away?"

"Oh, I don't know. Maybe the way you keep staring at the forest."

She glanced back at the ominous clump of trees that lined the right side of the path. Nothing but darkness was beyond the trail of flashlights. "Anything could be out there."

Dylan held his flashlight under his nose and pretended to cry. "I'm so scared."

She patted him playfully. "Not funny."

He switched sides so he was closest to the brush. "Fine. I'll stay by the big bad forest and defend you."

"My hero." She smiled, then blushed, and glanced away.

They walked a bit farther, with only the sound of their shoes plodding on the dirt floor. Melena fidgeted with a silver ring on her thumb, trying to think of something clever to say. *Nothing.* Her mind was blank.

She glanced back over shoulder. Chad and April had drifted too far back to see any longer. *This would be so much easier if she was with me.*

"So, do you like your dad?" Dylan asked.

Melena pushed back the desire to exhale in relief. "Yeah, he's a good guy."

Dylan swayed his flashlight in circles in front of them. "I never really knew my dad. He died in a boating accident when I was five. It's been just my mom, my sister, and me for a long time."

"I'm sorry."

He swatted at the air. "Don't be. I've been open about it for years. It's how I process."

Chad ran up behind Dylan and hopped on his back. Dylan leaned forward, managing to not topple over. "Warn me next time, man." He dropped Chad to the ground.

"Hey, either of you got any gum? My date says she needs a piece."

Melena giggled. "The girl always needs gum. Here." She dug in her pant pocket and handed him a stick of Juicy Fruit. "I'm always prepared."

"Like a Girl Scout." Chad saluted and flowed back to his date.

Melena laughed. "He's a bit of a character."

"You could say that." Dylan pivoted around and walked backward. "His dad is in the Navy. He used to be stationed in Florida. Chad and I went to the same high school for about a year, until his dad got transferred to San Diego." He stumbled a bit and glanced at the ground. "Guess walking backward in the dark is kind of dumb."

She grinned.

He flipped next to her again. "It was cool to know someone when I first moved here."

"How long have you been here?"

"A little over two months."

Funny. She hadn't seen him before camp. "Do you go to our church?"

"Last Sunday was the first time I visited." He ran the flashlight along the edge of the forest, then back to their feet. "I actually signed up for camp the morning we left."

"Really? That's cool." *Yeah, I'm a woman of many words. Very articulate.* "So, are you in school?"

He passed a hand through his hair. "Yeah, I'm taking a few courses at Mesa Community College right now, but I plan to transfer somewhere in the spring. Maybe State. Though SDSU wouldn't be my first choice."

She gazed at him in the moonlight. The nervousness had receded a bit, though her stomach was still in knots. "What was your first choice?"

"University of Miami. I was accepted there last year."

"Why didn't you go?" Her feet stumbled over a protruding rock and she toppled forward.

Dylan caught her hand and didn't let go. "Are you okay?"

Chills ran up her arm. She swallowed, afraid to speak. His hand was warm, rough, and enveloped hers. The hairs on her arms stood to attention. Her pulse raced. She worked to block out the foreign fingers and concentrate on their owner. *But he's holding my hand. A guy is holding my hand.*

"I'm okay." She cleared her throat. "So, why didn't

you go to Miami?"

"I wanted to stay with my mom and help her raise my little sister."

"How old is she?" *Yeah! My voice didn't crack.*

"Twelve." He brushed her fingers with his thumb.

She inhaled and almost forgot to exhale. A small bird scurried in front of them, then darted back in the dark. Melena pressed against him.

Dylan laughed. "Scared of a tiny quail?"

"Hey, it could have been a rabid quail with gnarly teeth."

"I don't think birds have teeth."

"That's what makes that quail so scary."

"Yeah, okay." His smile gleamed in the darkness. "So, back to the subject. What about you? What do you want to be when you grow up?"

"I start college in the fall. As for what I want to be?" A question she had heard and thought about more than she'd like to admit. She sighed. "No idea, but I really like art. Maybe I'll do something with that."

"I love art. Who's your favorite artist?"

Without hesitation, she said, "Van Gogh. I love the passion in his lines." Her shoulders rolled up as she pictured the copies of his paintings plastered on her wall at home. She took art every year of high school and in her senior year, she studied him in depth. "Have you seen any of his paintings?"

"Some."

"He's amazing. The hues he used in his paintings changed according to what was going on in his life at the time. For instance, his hayfields were originally painted free and golden, but when he went into the hospital, they turned dark and sinister."

"Yeah, he was crazy." He winked.

She dropped Dylan's hand and stared at him, wide-eyed and opened mouthed. "How can you say that? He was a genius."

He snickered sarcastically. "Yeah, he was exceptionally smart when he cut off his ear."

"Okay, so he had his demons, but come on." She grabbed his shirtsleeve. "His work is amazing."

"Why can't you like real artists like Picasso, Sickert, and Degas?"

"Ah, abstract absurdity." She swiped the air and turned back to the road. Their feet scuffed down the dirt path. She glanced at him. "So, you really don't like Van Gogh?"

He took her hand again and smiled. "Yeah, he's good. I just thought I'd give you a hard time."

"Well, I'll admit I'm impressed you know who Sickert and Degas are."

"My uncle is a painter and used to take us to museums a lot. It was a chance for my mom to get out of the house."

Melena gazed at his profile. She *was* impressed. Wait, more than that. At first she assumed he was just a big flirt. Now she knew. The guy had substance. To her, that was key. No doubt, he was a fisherman and she was hooked.

"So, what do you want to do when you grow up?" Melena asked.

He shrugged. "I like English and history. I don't know, maybe journalism. I'm starting undeclared, though my mom is really pushing me to pick a major."

"Why? You've got time."

"I guess parents are supposed to push us to make a

goal. It's their job. They don't want us to end up as garbage can tossers."

Melena laughed. "I believe the PC word is garbage can engineer."

"Oh." He smiled. "I stand corrected."

"Besides, I hear they make good money."

"Hey, maybe you're right." He nodded. "Maybe I'll just forget the whole college thing and join the disposal engineer crew."

"Life ambition."

He smiled. "And a good one at that. Just call me Oscar."

They dropped down the hill and lights from camp glittered in the distance. They were almost back to the cabins. *Bummer*. Melena frowned.

"So, where do you live?" he asked.

"Orange County."

He looked at her. "Orange County? I meant what town; I didn't expect you to say a different county."

"Yeah, we live in Fullerton near Disneyland."

"Well, that stinks." He glanced at her with a furrowed brow. "We'll be over what, two hours away from each other?"

"Actually, just one." She turned away to hide the smile that played on her lips. *He actually cares whether or not I'm around. He likes me.* Then she frowned. *Uh oh! He's right.* They'd be separated.

"The O.C., huh? Are you anything like those girls on the show?"

"No!" She shoved him playfully. "I hope not."

He laughed.

A gust of wind flowed around them and she suddenly regretted ditching her coat. Shivering, she let go of his hand and pulled the ends of her sleeves into her palms.

"Cold?"

"Yeah. A little."

He removed his jacket and wrapped it around her shoulders. A musky sent drifted to her nose. Her heart accelerated beneath the folds of leather. She blinked, trying to focus. "Thanks, but won't you be cold?"

"Nah, I was kind of hot anyway." Dylan reached to the ground, picked up a small rock, and tossed it into the dark trees. "So, if you live up north, how did you get mixed up with this bunch?"

She summoned a smile. "Well, my dad used to be a pastor and my mom lives just outside San Diego in Del Mar. I usually visit her in the summer and attend the church when I can." She played with the head of the zipper. "Most my friends live in the Anaheim area. Well, except for April. She usually tells me when they're doing something."

"Well, I hope you come around. I'd like to see you."

Her stomach did a cartwheel. She focused on the round spotlight on the dirt floor. Suddenly, she felt hot in his jacket. But no way would she remove it.

As they neared the camp, April bounded up alongside of them, smacking her gum. "Hey, there you two are. I couldn't see you back there."

"Where's Chad?" Dylan glanced over his shoulder without letting go of Melena's hand.

April blew a big bubble and let it pop. "Oh, he's talking to some guy. Something about a youth surf camp coming up in September."

The path ended in front of the cabins, and the

16

group swirled into a cluster of talking heads. April took notice of Melena and Dylan's joined hands and smirked.

Melena shot her a warning look. *Don't you dare embarrass me.*

"Okay, folks," Pastor Scott yelled over the commotion. "Call it a night. Curfew in twenty!"

Melena caught Dylan's eye. He didn't break their gaze, just held it for a moment. She swallowed. *Okay, you're awesome.* She leaned toward April, willing the butterflies to take ten, and whispered, "You go ahead. I'll meet up with you in a minute."

Her friend looked from Melena to Dylan and back to Melena. A grin spread across her features. She snapped her gum. "Okay. 'Night guys." She skipped up the stairs and out of sight behind the cabin door.

Melena allowed herself to be led by Dylan to a log a few feet away. He let go of her hand, sat, pulled one of his legs up, and stared out into the darkness without a word. His jaw was tight, his thoughts private.

Maybe he's mad. She took a seat and faced him. "Are you upset?"

He turned to her with a reassuring smile. "What, me? No way. Not with you here." He laced his fingers through hers. "No, I was thinking how I would make it up to see you a lot."

Her cheeks warmed. *Great, the annoying blush has returned. Maybe he can't tell in the dark.* "Well, I'm here all summer, so I still have a while until I have to go back."

"Cool." He smiled.

He was so warm. She closed her eyes, afraid to let go and wake up. It was as good as any dream she'd ever

17

had. *Better.* She imagined his firm chest against her cheek and the pounding of his heart. Her eyes shot open. A twist of panic shot through her gut. *What if he tries to kiss me? Of course, I want him to. Wait, no, I don't. Would I even know how? What if I stink?*

Scott cleared his throat a few feet behind them. "Say goodnight, Dylan. Curfew means lights out." Dylan nodded and Scott continued to another couple leaning against the cabin.

"Well…" Almost relieved, Melena stood, not sure what to do next. She stumbled back a few steps. "Guess I'd better go."

"Yeah, we wouldn't want you to get in trouble." He stepped back and shoved his hands in his pockets.

"Oh." She unwrapped herself from his jacket and held it out.

He shook his head. "Keep it for now."

A huge grin beamed across her face. She waved, spun around, and walked to the cabin in a daze. With her mind this full, she knew she wouldn't be able to fall asleep but she wasn't worried. April would be there to extract all the juicy details and Melena couldn't wait to comply.

Chapter Three

The alarm clock buzzed for the third time. Melena slammed her fist on the snooze button and pulled the sleeping bag over her head. She imagined Dylan standing over her, staring with his intense eyes, as she ran her hand through his hair and he leaned to kiss her. Her heart raced. No way did she want to get up. She wanted to remain snuggled in her sleeping bag with her dreams.

April hopped up and down on the foot of the bed. "Aren't you up yet?"

Melena peeked out.

April tossed a pair of rolled up socks at her head, then flopped to the mattress, and bounced to her feet.

"I'm working on it." She grabbed the cotton wad and tossed it back, just missing April's left ear. "I don't want to wake up from this dream."

"What dream is that?" April perched on the edge of her own bunk and pulled a cookie from a duffel bag.

Melena sat up with her hands at her chest, swooning. "The one where Dylan leans in to kiss me."

"Oh *that* dream." April laughed. "Yeah, I had the same one last night."

Melena tossed her pillow. April ducked and struck Scott's wife, Justine, in the face.

April and Melena exchanged pinched smiles. "Whoops. Sorry, Justine," Melena said.

Justine blinked. "Good morning to you, too."

"It wasn't on purpose. I promise."

"I'll live." Justine eyed Melena's pajamas. "You better get a move on, or you'll miss devotions."

April tugged on Melena's arm. "See."

"I'm up." Melena pivoted around, letting her feet touch the icy wood floor. She cringed.

Justine dropped a Bible on the bunk. "We found this in the dining hall."

Melena scooped up her prized NIV and smiled. "Thanks. It was a gift from my dad at graduation. I'd be bummed to lose it."

Justine nodded and left.

Melena placed it in her bag, then shuffled into the shower. Ten seconds in, and she screamed. "The water's freezing!"

"That's what you get for being the last one up," April called from outside the door. "Serves you right."

Melena endured as much of the glacier dip as she could stand, then stepped out, and into a yellow robe. She glanced in the mirror. Her purple lips confirmed how she felt. Shaking, she walked back to her bunk and retrieved her clothes. "Yeah, well, next year you can bet I'll get first shower." Her teeth chattered.

April laughed from the other side of the wall. "I doubt it."

"You'll see." Melena turned on her blow dryer before April could respond. She took extra long on her hair, curling the ends, and spraying every strand. She powdered her nose, put on mascara, and applied two layers of dewberry lipstick.

April chuckled at Melena's reflection. "You look like you're going to a wedding, instead of camp devotions."

Melena scowled. "I didn't do that much."

April raised an eyebrow.

She glanced back at her reflection. "You think I did too much?"

"You look great." She elbowed Melena, then fingered the end of her hair. "I really should grow my hair out. Yours is so pretty."

"You always say that." Melena studied her friend's short, punked-out style. "But you never do."

"I know. It's such a hassle. Once it gets past my shoulders, I don't know what to do with it. Maybe I'll just dye it again."

"Just not purple this time."

"Blue?" She giggled.

Melena shook her head. "Please don't. I won't be able to hang out with you in public."

"Ha! You're no fun." April grabbed her Bible from the top of her bunk and crossed to the door. "Wait! Gum." She patted her jeans frantically. "Gum. Do you have any?"

"I think I saw a pack under your make up bag."

"You're a lifesaver." She returned to the mirror to snatch her prized yellow pack and withdrew a piece. "Want some?"

"Nah. Let's go. We're already late."

They walked the short distance to the small chapel and stepped inside. Instantly, Melena's stomach danced. Dylan leaned against an usher's table in the back, looking incredible in a white surfer's tee, board shorts, and sandals.

She took a deep breath and walked toward him. *Don't freak out. Don't say anything dumb. Just smile and pray.* She bared her teeth and hoped she didn't look like the Joker in Batman.

"Hey there, good looking." Dylan took her hand and led her to a pew in front. "How'd you sleep?"

In hopes of retaining her olive complexion instead of the embarrassing ruby-red cheeks her best friend was always teasing her about, she studied the floor. "Okay, once I was able to fall asleep."

"Yeah, I thought about you all night, too."

A flood of fire lit under her skin. *Just look at April's shoulder and breathe.*

Luckily, Pastor Scott chose that moment to open the service.

****

After devotions and a quick cereal and Pop-Tart breakfast, Pastor Scott called them together for one final announcement session in front of the cabins. He stepped up on a wooden bench with a bullhorn and everyone fell silent. "Okay, everyone. I hope you had an amazing week."

The group offered the appropriate applause and cheers.

"Well, it's time to pack up and get down the mountain." He pulled a red flyer out of his back pocket and held it up. "As you know, it has been our tradition to end the summer with one more major event."

Feet shuffled, girls giggled, and guys elbowed the expectant announcement.

"This will be our third year hosting an end of the summer banquet. This year, the proceeds will go to aid Teen Challenge, so I hope you'll all come out and support this dinner." He folded the paper and smiled. "And bring a date!"

Everyone howled.

"Now, go pack. We're out of here in thirty." He jumped down and spun his finger around in a circle. "And go!"

People shuffled in all directions.

Melena turned to Dylan. "Guess I'll see you in a bit."

"Meet you at the bus." He winked, then joined the other guys.

Melena twisted around and skipped up the steps to her cabin. *End of the Summer Banquet.* She went every year, never with a date, usually with her brother Nick. The thought of Dylan in a tux made her giddy.

She pushed open the wood door. April glanced up from stuffing her sleeping bag in a black trash bag. "Okay, you've got to stop smiling."

Which only made Melena smile more.

"He's going to think you're a fruitcake."

"I can't help it." Melena tossed the last of her clothes in the suitcase and zipped it closed. "I just can't believe a good looking guy could actually like me."

"Why? You're hot!" Smiling, April ran her gaze over Melena's body, then wrapped her arm around her shoulders, and squeezed.

Melena laughed. She put the straps of her backpack over her arm and clutched the handle of her suitcase. "I'll see you on the bus?"

"No, I'm ready." April walked to the mirror, took one last look at her reflection, and said, "Let's blow this place."

They dropped their bags on the ground by the bus and a couple of guys threw them in the back of a pickup truck. Melena made hearts with her feet in the dirt while they waited for the guys to join them. "So, what do you think of Chad?"

April beamed. "*Hello!* If I didn't have a boyfriend already, he'd be mine."

"He's cute."

She smiled. "No, he's hot and SO like me. I've never met a guy with his humor. We actually get each other."

Melena spotted them over April's shoulder a few feet away. "Shh! Here they come."

"Hi." Dylan pitched his bag with the rest of them and tickled Melena's side.

She squirmed away. "Hi, yourself."

He grabbed her hand and escorted her to the bus door. "Ready to go?"

"Ready." She smiled and stepped up.

On the bus, Melena slid into a seat in the back row and Dylan sat in the seat next to hers. Chad and April filled in next to them. Melena stared out the window, disappointed. The rest of the campers piled their bags in the truck and moved to leave. When the last person was on the bus, Dylan tapped April on the shoulder and motioned for them to switch places.

Melena's heart skipped with joy and relief. She smiled as he took her hand.

The bus rolled forward. Dylan edged closer and whispered, "I like that you're always smiling."

"You make me smile." She glanced away, bidding her cheeks to remain cool.

"I'd like to hang out when we get back." He toyed with the turquoise ring on her pinkie, then lured her gaze. "Maybe get dinner or go to the beach."

Her stomach somersaulted. *Oh my! Just breathe.*

She pinched her lips together to keep from screaming. *Absolutely!*

His eyes searched hers.

She grinned. "I'd like that, too."

They rode the rest of the trip in a comfortable silence. At one point, she laid her head on his shoulder and fell asleep. When she woke, his gaze was focused on her. "I must have dozed off. Hope I didn't snore." *Did I just say that out loud?*

He shook his head and opened his mouth to say something, when the bus stopped.

"Grab your gear," Pastor Scott said. Everyone in front of them scrambled off. Dylan stood and motioned for her to go in front of him. She grabbed her backpack and shifted down the narrow aisle, then outside the door. The group waited by the truck for their bags to be unloaded. Melena found her stuff and moved toward April's lime-green bug.

Dylan walked over to her with a duffel bag draped over his shoulder. "Can I get your phone number?"

Melena dug out her cell phone and glanced at the screen. *Oh no! It's dead. Why did I leave it on all week? It wasn't like there was any service.* "Um, my phone is dead."

"We can do it old school." He smiled. "Do you have a pen?"

She searched around in her backpack for a pen. *I know there is one in here somewhere.* Her finger touched something long and thin. She pulled it out. *Drat! A pack of gum.* She started to put it back in when April snatched it out of her hand.

"Thanks, friend."

Melena shook her head and shoved her hand back

in the bag. Her hand grazed something skinny and plastic. *Yes.* She withdrew eyeliner. *Ah!* "Sorry."

He laughed and pulled a Sharpie from his duffel bag. "Here," he said, handing it out.

She took it, then seized his hand, and wrote her number on his palm.

He studied it for a moment, then smiled. "Cool." He opened his arms for a hug and she filled them. The spicy scent of cologne lingered even after he pulled back. Adrenaline pumped through her heart.

"Bye." Dylan waved and walked to where Chad waited beside a red truck.

Melena climbed in April's car, but kept her eyes diverted in his direction. He met her gaze, smiled, and winked.

April slammed her door shut as she popped her bubble and started the car. The engine roared to life. "You've really got it bad. Don't you, Mel?" She turned out of the parking lot and Dylan went out of sight.

Melena faced the road and sighed. *I just hope he calls.*

Chapter Four

Dylan pulled up in front of the brown apartments and shut off the engine. He could hear the bass of his sister's angry-girl rock from the street. *Mom really needs to address that.* He lifted the duffel bag from the back and slammed the door shut with his foot.

His mom must have seen him drive up, because she met him on the front step. "Welcome back, son." She stood on her tiptoes to kiss his cheek.

"Hey, Mom." He walked past her into the house and set his stuff down in the entryway. The walls and his mom's ceramic collection vibrated from the stereo above. "You can hear her music from the street."

"Yeah, I keep telling her to turn it down," she said, shutting the screen door.

Dylan plugged his ears and pretended to yell. "I'm sorry, what did you say?"

She patted his arm. "I'll talk to her again."

"Thank you."

"You know what they say?" his mom said.

He cocked his head to the side. "No, what's that?"

"If the music is too loud, you're getting old." She smiled and turned for the stairway.

Dylan shook his head, then grabbed his stuff, and dropped it in the study. The large room doubled as his room and his mom's office. He didn't mind. It wasn't like he was there much anyway. Usually, Chad talked

27

him into going somewhere and he had plans to get a job soon. Not to mention, now there was Melena.

A big smile encompassed his face. Yeah, he'd happily give his days to her. He kicked back on the sofa bed and sighed. She was pretty, sweet, and didn't get offended by his odd sense of humor. He thought about the way her bright brown eyes danced when she talked about Van Gogh and how her high cheekbones betrayed her when he flirted. Her slightly crooked smile that almost always beamed and her lean body that suggested she was athletic.

He turned on his phone and scrolled over his apps. Nothing interested him. His eyes glazed over, and he realized the screen was a blur against the woman in his mind. There was a mysterious quality about her he couldn't quite pinpoint.

He stared at the number written on his hand and wondered if he should call her. *No, it's too early. I just left her. She'll think I'm nuts.* He dropped his phone on the table and rolled over to stare at the wood ceiling. He couldn't wait to see her again.

****

"So, you get any lip?" April asked, as they exited the highway.

"What?" Melena gasped. "No!"

April laughed. "Why not?"

"April, come on. You know my past. I've never even held a guy's hand before this weekend."

She shook her head. "I told you your biological clock is ticking. Eighteen years old and you've just now held a guy's hand. Come on, Mel. I was like ten."

Melena narrowed her eyes. "Yeah, and that's made your life so much better. How many toads have you

28

kissed?"

"Touché, but don't get mad." April pulled in Melena's driveway and shut off the engine. "I'm glad he's into you. He seems like a cool guy."

Melena smiled—again. "Yeah, he is."

"Well, I'll stop by later. Maybe we can go do something."

"Okay." Melena grabbed her stuff from the trunk, waved, then lugged her suitcase to the front of her house. Jiggling the knob with her free fingers, she managed to push the door open. "Mom? I'm home."

No response. The house appeared empty, yet the door was unlocked. *Hmm?* She set her bags down and closed the door. In the dimly lit house, a downpour of sadness washed over her. Melena wished she was still at camp. April called it "letdown"—the moment when fun was over and reality emerged.

The red light blinked on the answering machine in the entryway. She pushed play.

"Melena, it's your dad. I hope you had a fun week. Give me a call. I think I'll be picking you up a week earlier. Kevin has to be back for soccer practice. Bye, hon."

The message turned off. How she missed him. She reached to call him and realized the receiver wasn't in the charger. She pushed the button and followed the beep. It rested on the kitchen counter. She snatched it and dialed the familiar number. "Dad?"

"Sweetheart. Good to hear from you. How was camp?"

"Great." *Awesome! Amazing! The best week of my life.* Melena slid onto a stool and leaned forward on her elbows. "I just got back. How are Nick and Kevin?"

"Good. Did you get my message?"

She nodded as if he could hear her head rattle. "Just let me know when I should pack."

"I'll call you with the exact day, but for now, plan for early August."

Melena frowned. *Less time here with Dylan.* "Okay, Dad."

"Love you and miss you."

She smiled. "I love you, too, Dad. Bye."

"Bye, sweetheart."

Melena hung up and sighed. *I'm exhausted.* She hadn't slept much the night before. *But it was so worth it.* She went back into the entryway, grabbed her bags, and dragged them up the stairs to her room. The space looked exactly as she'd left it. Piles of CDs and books lined the charcoal gray walls. The glass desk was cluttered with penciled sketches. Volleyball equipment peeked out from under the bed. The blinds were drawn over the bay window, and rejected outfits for the camping experience were scattered among her blankets.

She released her bags and smiled. A magazine copy of Van Gogh's *Starry Night* stared at her from over the bed. The memory of Dylan's teasing about his sanity made her laugh. She flopped face down on the bed, exhausted. Too bad she hadn't met Dylan on Monday. What a different week it would have been. But, of course, there was still over a month of summer left. *Plenty of time to get together with him.* In her mind's eye, his radiant smile glimmered at her, drawing her to him. She rolled over, grabbed the pillow, and pulled it against her face. "Aah!"

The melodic tune from her cell phone rang from downstairs. Why did she leave it there? She shot forward, tumbled off her bed, and darted down the stairs to the living room phone. "Hello?" she said winded.

"Hi, Melena?"

Her heart skipped a beat. "Dylan?"

"Dylan? No, it's Nick. *Your brother*."

She frowned. "Oh, hi, Nick."

"Don't sound so thrilled."

"Sorry." She closed her eyes and wilted to the couch. "What's up?"

He cleared his throat. "I called to talk to Brian, I must have hit your number by accident. Is he home?"

Their stepfather, Brian, had married their mother the day after their parents' divorce was final. Though Melena was young, she remembered Brian coming around way before her parents even said the "D" word. For that reason alone, she had never fully accepted him.

"I didn't see his car in the driveway. Want me to leave a message for him?"

"Nah, I can call him." He paused for a second, and then said, "Hey, Kevin wants to say hello, okay?"

"Yeah, put him on." She adored her baby brother, especially since she helped raise him.

"Hi, Sis. How's the weather down there?"

"Perfect, as always. How's Dad treating you?"

"Oh, he chains me in the basement and makes me feed his pet rats," Kevin said.

"Yeah, I hate it when he does that." They both laughed. "When am I going to see you again?"

"Unless you come see me, probably when we make the switch in August." His voice squeaked. "Look, I've got to go. Nick needs to use the phone. Tell Mom and Cassi I love them. I'll see you soon." She couldn't believe his voice was starting to change. Every year, he shot up while they were apart, and it frustrated her. Divorce frustrated her.

"Okay, take care and give Dad a big hug for me."

"Bye, Sis."

She tapped the call off and sighed. Melena loved her brothers. Nick was sixteen and took after their father in every way—his looks and his sense of humor. Blond hair, high cheekbones, and olive skin, Melena and he could have been twins. Appearance aside, they'd always been close.

Her sister and she were more than a different story. If Melena was romance, her sister would be science fiction. They had had a surly relationship basically since Cassandra had learned to talk. Cassi was now fourteen, going on twenty-five. She took after their mother not only in looks, but also in the ability to manipulate everyone around her. She had shoulder length, chocolate-brown hair, ivory skin, and cool-blue eyes. No one would have ever guessed Melena and Cassi were sisters. Thirteen-year-old Kevin, however, tied them all together. He had golden-brown hair with blue eyes, fair skin, and high cheekbones. He was, in all ways, the neutral one.

The kids all moved in with their father when their parents separated. That lasted until their mother remarried. Once she had a new husband, she took their father back to court for joint custody. Melena didn't really like living with her mother, so she only came down for a few months in the summer. Her mother complained to her face, but Melena was convinced it was only a ruse.

Melena's stomach rumbled. With all the nerves,

she hadn't eaten in twenty-four hours. She went into the kitchen and inspected the contents of the refrigerator. A big meal sounded awful. She just needed to get something in her body. A cup of peach yogurt caught her eye. She grabbed it, dumped it in a bowl, and sprinkled granola over it. As she took a bite, she reflected on the week.

The main theme had been about building relationships. Melena knew it was what she needed to hear, but she had a long way to go. Things were not exactly like the show *Happy Days* in her home. At camp, Melena had prayed for a new start.

The cherry on top of her week was, of course, Dylan. She smiled to herself. It was a good thing no one was around to see her sitting here smiling. They'd probably think she was crazy. She scraped the final bite from her bowl as Cassi pushed through the kitchen's white French doors wearing ultra low-ride jeans and a tight pink T-shirt bearing the word "Princess."

"Good morning."

Cassi eyed her. "Yeah, whatever."

"What's wrong with you?"

"Nothing's wrong." She sneered. "Just because some of us aren't Pollyanna in the morning, doesn't mean something's wrong."

Unbelievable. You aren't going to make this easy, are you, Lord? "It's after eleven."

"Your point?" Cassi tossed her purse on the kitchen table and reached for a croissant. "Where's Mom?"

"It's Saturday. Probably at work."

"Good." Cassi peeled off a layer of the bread and popped it in her mouth. "Look, I have some friends coming over later and you'd better not say anything to Mom."

Melena raised an eyebrow. "And if I do?"

She stepped forward, eyes narrowed, hands on hips. "I'll make your life miserable."

Melena snickered and turned to rinse her bowl. "You already do."

"Ha! Don't test me, Melena. You know I can be the queen of nasty." She bit into her croissant but kept her eyes on her sister.

True. Cassi was an evil brat. Actually, another word came to mind, but Melena was too Christian to go there. Truthfully, she didn't understand her sister. *Why does she dress like that? And what makes her talk to people so rudely?* Most encounters with her sister ended in questions.

Cassi slid on a stool and flipped open a teen magazine.

Melena stared at her. *Why does she act so spoiled? Why can't she be more like Nick and me?* But she knew the answer. *Mom.* Their mom had spoiled her from the crib. Something their father despised, but with her parents' waning relationship, his opinion didn't go far. It was a wonder Kevin had turned out okay.

Melena dropped her dishes in the dishwasher, grabbed a bottle of water, and started to leave.

Cassi's gaze followed her. "So you aren't going to say anything, right?"

Melena glanced back at her sister. "You shouldn't go behind Mom's back."

"Why do you care?"

"Because it's not right."

Cassi puckered her lips in a defiant stare. "It's not a

34

big deal, Melena. Just a few friends."

"Good, then it won't matter if I say anything." Melena unscrewed the lid off her water and crossed to the stairs.

"You're such a goodie-two-shoes."

"Thank you," Melena yelled back.

Cassi harrumphed and mumbled some questionable words under her breath.

Melena didn't care. She was used to making her sister mad. So with a shrug, she skipped upstairs to her room and shut the door. The room felt empty. *What do I feel like doing?* A bit of after-event letdown started to creep into her emotions. She sat on her bed and dug under the mattress for her leather journal, hopefully a place free from prying eyes. When she was sixteen, Cassi had found it, ripped out some of the pages, and handed them out at school. *I'm sure the fifth graders were thrilled.*

Melena withdrew a pen attached to the side, then thumbed to an empty page. *July 8th.* A big grin plastered her face. *Where do I even begin?* She tapped the pen against her lips. "Hmm?" She brought it to the paper, when someone knocked at the door.

"Come in."

April bounded in and laughed. "Are you still smiling?"

"Can't help it. I'm gone."

"I'll say." She shook her head.

Melena stuffed her journal under her bed and flipped around to face her friend. "What are you up to? I didn't expect you this quick."

April plopped on a beanbag in the corner and exhaled along with the chair. "No one was home, and it was lonely. I thought maybe we could go get some food or something."

"Aren't you tired?"

"Nah." She slapped at the air. "Just craving good French fries in a big way."

"Fries? Why?"

Her nose turned up. "Those camp fries were nasty. Tasted like dish soap or something."

Melena laughed. "Fine. I'm game. Just let me throw on something else." She examined her hands. Dirt lined the cracks in her fingers and nail beds. "Actually, give me a few minutes to wash up."

April eyed her dusty jeans and faded orange T-shirt that read, *If you're living like there's no God, you'd better be right.* "What's wrong with going the way you are?"

Melena shook her head and grabbed a blue T-shirt from the closet along with a pair of jeans. "I promise. I won't take long." She stepped down the hall to the bathroom. Her face was oily and smudges of dirt lined her jaw. A warm shower was just what she needed—a far cry from the glacier falls of that morning. She let the blanket of steam ease her nerves. She wanted to stay, but knew April would drag her out if she made her friend wait too long. April wasn't exactly the most patient person. Melena turned off the water, dried, and pulled on the clean clothes.

When she returned to the room, April was thumbing through her closet. "You have so many clothes and I don't think I've seen you in half of them." She held up a Navy baby-doll shirt to her chest and stepped to the mirror. "This is cute."

Melena snatched it out of her hand and hung it

back on the rack. "Don't even think about it. Last time you borrowed something of mine, it ended up in a vat of mud."

"Hey, can I help it if I'm a klutz? Besides, who knew it would rain that day?"

"Or that you couldn't walk in those high heels?"

April rolled her eyes. "Whatever, Mel."

Melena laughed. "Yeah, well, I'm counting on your ill-fated luck. Don't mess with my clothes."

"Most of these outfits won't see a minute out of your closet." April fingered the sleeve of a silver jacket. "They're lonely. They need out."

"That's because my mom bought them in some vain effort to make me stylish. I'm no Cassi."

"Thank goodness." April slid the closet door closed. "Are you ready?"

Melena nodded. "Let's bounce."

They went to a café a few blocks from her house. Melena ordered a Cobb salad with no tomatoes and extra dressing. April got a burger with extra cheese and a family-size plate of fries.

"You praying, or am I?" April said.

Melena shrugged. "Go ahead."

April blessed the food and said, "Amen," as the waitress placed their plates in front of them. She visibly breathed in the smell of the fries. "Ah, yes."

"Can you pass the pepper?" Melena said.

April handed it to her and leaned in. "Guess what?"

"What?"

"We've been invited to a beach party at Pastor Scott's house tomorrow night."

"Really? Who's invited?" Melena poured blue cheese dressing over her food and mixed everything together.

"The whole gang from camp and some of the youth group." April squished chewed gum on the side of her glass and bit the end off a French fry. She closed her eyes. "Mmm…that's good."

Melena laughed. "You mean, Dylan?"

"Precisely."

Melena's heart fluttered and, suddenly, she didn't feel hungry. She set the fork on the table and sat back. "Go on."

"I hear you just walk out their backdoor and you're on the beach. They plan to barbecue. It'll be a blast."

"Count me in." Melena took a sip of lemonade and wished it were twenty-four hours later.

April started her ritual of drowning her fries in ketchup, sweetening her tea, saturating her bun with mustard, and placing a napkin in her lap. When she was apparently ready to eat, she asked, "Has Dylan called yet?"

Melena laughed. "You're worse than me. It's only been a few hours."

"Wow, that long?" April smiled. "He'll call."

Staring at the bacon, avocado, and blue cheese mixture, Melena secretly hoped so. He liked her, right? *Of course, he does.* The thought of her friend, Patricia, flashed through her mind. Two summers ago, she had met a guy at camp and he never talked to her again. They had even kissed. Melena lifted her fork and stabbed a crouton. *But Dylan's different. He'll call. I mean, why wouldn't he?*

"Earth to Melena."

She peered up. "Sorry, guess I'm just doing my worry thing."

"God and chocolate. That's all you need."

Melena giggled. Her friend could be impossible at times, but she loved the girl for the times April made her laugh. "Then I guess I need a double chocolate brownie a la mode."

"Yes! With whipped cream and nuts." April lifted her hand in the air. "Waitress."

Chapter Five

Sunday afternoon, Melena dug through her straw laundry basket in search of something to wear. Already, she'd tried on four pairs of shorts and at least ten T-shirts. She turned sideways in the full-length mirror and frowned. She was eighteen, but still had the figure of a twelve-year-old. Skinny—desperately without curves. Her sister was the one blessed with the chest and hips. Both of which were always exposed by tight layers of clothing. *I'm the modest one. Why couldn't I have the figure?*

She grabbed a pair of olive-green street shorts from her bed and stepped into them. They made her legs look long and tan. *Yeah, these will work.* She spotted a camouflage tee peeking out from her drawer. *Perfect.* She slipped it on, then dug in her closet for her brown-wedge sandals. *There they are.* She slipped them on, then vamped at her reflection. "Dylan, eat your heart out." She laughed and glanced around the room, then bounded down the stairs and to the door.

Just as she reached for the handle, the phone rang. She started to dismiss it, but changed her mind. She opened the door again and walked in to hear the message machine beep off. *Drats!* She pushed play and smiled at the sound of Dylan's voice. "Hi, Melena. This is Dylan. The guy you met at camp."

She giggled.

"Sorry it took me so long to call you. I actually lost your cell number, but I found your landline online. I mean, I hope this is you. Anyway..." He chuckled. "I just hope I'll get to see you at the party tonight. If not, I'll call you tomorrow. Bye." She pushed play again and held her hands to her chest. *He called.* She started to listen to it again, when she noticed the time. *Got to go.* She glanced at the machine. *See you soon.*

The unmasked sun was bright in the sky. A soft haze fell over the city, exhibiting the lack of rain and the overdose of pollution. The air was searing and dry from the Santa Ana winds blowing in from the desert.

She pulled her blue Honda Accord into April's driveway and shut off the engine. Disgruntled voices emanated from inside the two-story house. Melena walked up the cobblestone path to the side door and knocked. No one answered. She turned the knob and peeked in.

"But, Mom, that's not fair. It's Jenny's mess, not mine," April cried.

"April Noel, I really don't care. If I don't see that mess in the backyard cleaned up by the time I return, you will spend the rest of the summer in this room. Do you understand?"

"Mom, I'm eighteen. You can't do this."

"I can as long as you want to stay under my roof."

Melena tipped-toed through the kitchen, up the stairs, and parked in the dark bathroom doorway.

"You spent all of last week at some camp, then expect to come back here, and skip out on your chores. You need to rethink your priorities, young lady. Now, get started." April's mom slammed the door and stomped in the bathroom. Flipping on the light switch, she jumped. "Um…Melena, what are you doing in here?"

Melena's cheeks warmed. "I'm sorry. I didn't want to interrupt you two."

"I see. Well, I'm afraid April won't be able to go to your party tonight. I'm sorry." She offered a tight grin, then stormed down the stairs, and out the front door.

Melena walked to April's room and found her friend face down, crying into her pillow. "Hi." She placed a hand on her friend's back. "I'm sorry, April."

April wiped her eyes and forced a smile. "Oh, hey. I didn't hear you come in." She sniffed. "Any word from Dylan yet?"

Melena shook her head and sat next to her on the bed. "Are you okay?"

She unrolled a few sheets of toilet paper from the roll in her lap. "Fine, but embarrassed. I'm supposed to be an adult." She paused to blow her nose, then laughed. "I'm sure the whole block knows I'm really not."

Melena pouted and pulled her friend into a hug. "At least your mom shows she cares. I can't remember the last time me and mine had it out."

"Not feeling better." April sniffed.

"Sorry."

April looked up and dabbed at her eyes, then wiped her nose. "Well, it's probably better I don't go."

"Why's that?"

April imparted a slight grin. "It will keep me true to Seth."

Her boyfriend, Seth, lived eight hours away in Tucson, Arizona. They'd been together for over a year, but she only saw him when he came to visit his grandma about every three months. Doing the math, they'd actually hung out four or five times during their entire relationship.

"When are you going to end this long distance thing? You hardly ever see him." Melena pushed her friend's hair away from her eye. "Besides, you're always scoping out other guys."

"He plans to enlist in the Navy in May, so he'll be moving down here after I graduate."

"Really?"

"Really. So, I have to be true to him." She grinned through her tears.

"Okay." Melena patted her leg. "Well, since we're not going to the party, we'd better get to work on your yard before your drill-mama returns."

April's eyes went wide. "What do you mean *we*? You're still going."

"No, I'm not."

"Yes, you are."

"*No*, I'm not." Melena crossed her arms. "I'm staying here to help my best friend clean."

April shook her head emphatically. "Don't be absurd, Mel. Dylan is going to be there."

She shrugged. "I'm sure I'll see him another time. He's going to call tomorrow."

"I know you better than that." April clutched her friend's arm and stared into her eyes. "You *want* to see him."

Melena played with the hem of her shirt. Of course, she wanted to see him, but she was too petrified to go alone. She pressed her hands against her face in the image of Munich's *Scream*. "I'm scared."

"Don't do that. It's ugly and will give you

wrinkles." April pulled her friend's hands down. "I don't understand why you'd be nervous. You got along famously the other day on the bus."

Melena snorted. "Ha! Didn't you notice how much time we spent *not* talking? We spoke maybe a dozen words on the ride home."

"You slept half of it."

Melena nodded once. "Yeah, for that reason."

"Okay…" April waved her hand. "But you talked on the night hike."

"That was different. It was dark."

April raised an eyebrow. "Why is it different? He likes you. You like him. Who cares what you talk about? He's just a guy. Granted, a really cute guy." She smiled. "But one just the same." She took hold of Melena's hand and squeezed. "You have to go. You'll regret it if you don't."

Melena pinched her eyes shut. *Can I actually do this? Go by myself.* "Okay," she whispered.

April slapped her back. "That's my girl. Now, jet. The party starts soon."

Melena scooted back and got to her feet. "If I make it out alive, I'll call you tomorrow and let you know how it went."

April laughed. "You'd better."

Melena backed up slowly. Her nerves wavered.

"I promise. You'll be fine." April stood and escorted her to the stairs, then out the door.

As Melena climbed in the car, the thought of seeing Dylan electrified her heart rate. She glowed as she started the engine. *Tonight is going to be the coolest night ever! I hope.*

Chapter Six

Melena followed her GPS and arrived at the address a little past five. She slowed at the house and glanced around. The side streets surrounding the house were packed with cars. *Great.* She allowed the car to roll forward as she scoured for a spot. *Nothing.* Speeding up, she drove around the block a few times before deciding to park farther down the beach. After parking, she grabbed her beach towel and backpack from the trunk. The security lock on her car beeped as she started her trek to the party. She traipsed through a mile of sand, up a dozen steps, and down a small walkway before arriving at the private beach property.

The front of the house faced the street and the rear hung over the water on stilts. She could hear music and laughter, but a rock wall blocked her view. She glanced around. Steps ran along the side of the house. *Great, more climbing.* She walked up the rickety wood stairway that ended at a stained-glass door. A clay pelican perched on a weathered wood railing. The house reminded her of an old Popeye cartoon, which strangely gave her courage as she rapped on the door.

Justine answered with a smile. "Hi. I'm glad you came. Come in."

Melena stepped inside. The smell of popcorn and fresh baked cookies drifted to her nose. She glanced around the deserted condo. A red leather couch sat in

45

the middle of the room. Red and black abstract art decorated two white walls. The other two walls were glass, overlooking the sea.

Justine shut the door. "Where's April?"

"She couldn't make it."

"Well, I'm glad you came. We miss seeing you around."

"Yeah." Melena shifted her weight. "Thanks for inviting me. I had a really nice time at camp."

She smiled. "Yes, it was an amazing week. Seems you made a new friend?"

Melena felt her face warm. "Um…yeah…how do I get down to the party?"

"Through there." Justine pointed to a sliding glass door just off the living room. "Take off your shoes and I'll show you."

"Thanks." Melena looked down at the white carpet and took hold of her sandals.

They walked through the opening and down more steps to the beach. Lanterns and torches lined the sand. A group of youth surrounded a long table covered with food. A bonfire roared in the middle of the party, a small group of boys played volleyball a few yards away, a couple talked quietly on some rocks to her left, and another group of girls giggled to her right.

"Get something to eat if you'd like. I've got to get some cookies out of the oven." She patted Melena's shoulder and left.

Melena searched the faces. From what she could see, it appeared none of her friends had come yet. *But there's always my true love—volleyball.* A smile touched her mouth and grew until her cheeks ached. She walked over to a guy who had just bumped a ball over the net.

"Hey, can I play?"

The tall guy with bushy hair glanced her way. "Yeah, we need a third. Take the set."

She dropped her shoes and towel and took her place at the net. "I'm Melena."

"Ken," the redhead said. "He's Mick."

A portly guy with sideburns nodded. She remembered seeing him at camp.

Ken served and the other team spiked it back. Melena blocked it over for a point.

"Yes!" Ken pumped his fist. "You looked like you played."

Did my boyish figure give it away?

Her team won the first game and lost the second. As she started to duck under the net, she saw him. *Dylan.* "I think I'm going to take a break."

Ken frowned. "You can't leave. We haven't won the match yet."

She smiled. "Thanks for letting me play." She waved and turned away, but not before catching Ken's pout.

Melena smiled. It felt good to play again. She grabbed her stuff from the sideline and started in Dylan's direction. She snapped to a halt. Her smile fell.

What's she doing here?

Chapter Seven

Melena blinked. Dylan sat with his arm draped over the back of Cassi's lawn chair. *Why is she even here? She didn't go to camp. She doesn't even go to youth group.* He leaned and whispered something in her ear. She laughed and whispered something back.

Fury raged through Melena's mind and down her back. This isn't happening. She narrowed her eyes. *Why is my guy with her?* He's smarter than that. Her lips twisted in disgust. *She's fourteen, Dylan. Fourteen. Jailbait.* She bit her lip. *Melena, just breathe.* She was losing control. After a week at camp giving her anger to God, it was about to detonate. *I'm sure there is a logical explanation.*

He wore a cap backward on his head and a white T-shirt revealed his tight, muscular chest. *Why do you have to look so good?* For a second, his eyes turned her direction. Her stomach flipped. He didn't seem to notice her. *Or pretended not to.*

Almost in slow motion, Cassi's hand stroked his bicep.

Melena gritted her teeth and paced a few feet back. *I should pray, walk away, cool down.* But her flawed human psyche didn't care about *shoulds*. It cared about *wants*. Right now, she wanted Cassi to plunge in the ocean and Dylan to drape his arm around her instead.

Melena watched them in the shadow of the house.

The sun dipped behind the ocean without the two of them breaking once from their conversation. *I need to just leave.* A lump lodged in her throat and she batted her eyelids to keep from crying. She stood and brushed the sand from her shorts. *One more glance and I'm out of here.*

Someone tapped on her shoulder.

"Hey, Melena."

Melena turned around and wiped at her eyes. "Chad. Hi."

"Where's April?"

"Um...she's in a bit of trouble at home and couldn't get away."

He frowned. "That's too bad."

"Yeah." She glanced back at Dylan. He still hadn't looked away from Cassi. "Well, I'm going to take off."

"You sure? We're getting ready to play another game of volleyball. We could use another body, and I hear you're pretty good."

She shook her head. "Maybe some other time."

"Okay, see you, Melena."

"Bye."

Chad sauntered past her to Dylan. "Hey, man. Want to play some v-ball?"

Cassi looked up and brushed a strand of hair out of her eyes. Like a beacon in the night, a silver bracelet dangled from her right wrist.

My birthday gift from April! A bomb in Melena's chest exploded. Without acknowledging Dylan, she marched up to Cassi with jaded eyes. "Give me my bracelet."

"Melena, hi." Dylan smiled and stood. "When did you get here?"

"Almost two hours ago." She glanced at him, rolled her eyes, and looked back at her sister. "Give it back, Cassi."

"Can't you see I'm busy?" She rose and pawed Dylan's arm. "You know, Melena, people are going to wonder who the older sister is."

Dylan stepped free of Cassi and said to Melena, "Can we talk?"

Melena glanced at him and back to her sister. "After I get my bracelet back."

"Why don't you give her bracelet back, okay?" he said.

"Fine." Cassi placed her right hand over the chain and tugged. It broke, sending charms flying in all directions. She covered her smirk with her other hand. "Whoops. So, sorry."

Melena gasped, then stepped toward her sister with an extended finger. "You're asking for it."

Cassi fixed her with a defiant stare. "What are you going to do about it? You don't have it in you to do anything. Do you, Melena? Poor, helpless Melena." Cassi pushed out her lower lip, doe-eyed. "Shy and boring."

Without thinking, Melena grabbed a piece of chocolate cake from the end of the table and smeared it in Cassi's face.

Her sister's eyes grew round. She sputtered and staggered back, wiping at the frosting on her left cheek. "No, you didn't!" She seized a bowl of ambrosia salad and hurled it at Melena.

It landed in her hair.

Someone yelled, "Two points."

Melena countered with a handful of onion dip to

Cassi's shirt.

They began grabbing whatever food was closest. A rain of chips, cookies, cake, and dip filled the air. A bowl of salsa just missed Dylan's shoulder. Melena paused just long enough to see him duck out of the way and step back.

Goop poured down Melena's face. She wiped at it with a wet arm and blinked to see.

Four courses later, a crowd had formed around them. Cheers erupted from the Cassi clones.

Melena rushed at her sister.

Pastor Scott jumped in and sprayed them with a hose. "Enough!"

"Okay—" Melena blocked the spray with her forearm and dropped the melon in her hand.

"Look at what you've done to me, you jerk," Cassi huffed and turned on her heel for the stairway.

Melena flung her hands at the sand. Her clothes clung to her skin and her hair dripped down her face. Food seeped in every cranny of her body.

"What's wrong here?" Pastor Scott said. "We just got back from camp and talking about family relationships."

"It's a long story." Melena's voice cracked. "I'm sorry." She took in the sea of faces, some amused, others appalled. "I'll clean up."

Dylan stepped from the shadows. "I'll help, too."

Melena shot him a look of disdain, then diverted her gaze. She was in no mood to talk to him. Her anger still boiled at the image of him flirting with her sister.

"Melena," he said.

She scooped pieces of sandy melon into an empty bowl, not able to meet his eyes. It took everything in her to keep from crying. "I can't talk right now."

"Okay." True to his word, he helped, despite her cold reception. *Why? Shouldn't he follow Cassi? Make sure she's okay.* She grimaced.

After an hour of cleaning the trough, Dylan bowed out. Melena watched him climb the stairs with slumped shoulders. He turned back and met her gaze. She held it for a moment, then went back to cleaning. After he was gone, Melena apologized once again to her hosts and left herself.

The hike back to her car seemed to take forever. The air nipped at her arms and the dark streets felt foreboding. She just wanted to get home. As soon as she got in the car, a surge of tears flowed. She hadn't even acknowledged Dylan. Emotion welled in her chest, and she struggled to breathe. She really liked him. *He'll think I'm an idiot.* She reached for a napkin in the glove compartment and sobbed. What did it matter? He liked her sister. She started the engine. *Whatever Cassi wants, she gets.* It was the same ending every time. *I go home dripping in sorrow and Cassi is left to gloat.*

****

Dylan sat in his car and watched Melena step from the house and start to walk down the beach. He stepped out and started for her, but stopped. She obviously wasn't in the mood to talk. Why was she so angry? *Obviously, there is an issue with her sister, but why is she mad at me?*

He shook his head and climbed back in his car. It was a shame, too. He'd really looked forward to hanging out with her tonight. At first, he was excited when he ran into Cassi. He had drilled her for information about her sister. Maybe that was it. Maybe Melena didn't like him hanging around with her sister. *Oblivious to the obvious. Isn't that what people keep telling me?* He sighed. Maybe he could call Melena in the morning. Hopefully, she'd talk to him.

****

The drive home was a blur. Melena pulled in the driveway, staggered to the bathroom, showered, and flopped to bed. All she wanted to do was sleep and forget everything. But sleep eluded her. Replaying the night over and over, she watched the clock turn every hour. Dylan had seemed surprised she was there. But then, he probably felt caught. Images of Cassi and Dylan laughing made her cringe. "Aah!" She flipped on her belly and covered her head with the pillow. *Sleep. Please brain; put me out of my misery and let me sleep.*

Around six in the morning, she finally dozed off.

Suddenly, loud punk music blared from her stereo. She jolted awake.

Her sister stood at the foot of her bed, arms crossed, foot tapping.

"Turn it down." Melena thrust the pillow over her head.

"*Get* up." Cassi tugged on the comforter, then tried to yank Melena's pillow away. "I need to talk to you."

"I'm not in the mood." Melena repositioned her pillow. "Especially for you."

"Too bad. I want to know why you acted like such a wench last night."

"What? Sorry, I can't hear you."

Cassi yanked the pillow free and onto the floor. "What was your major deal last night?"

"Sorry, what was that?"

Cassi stomped over to the stereo and turned it off. "I said…why'd you act like such a jerk last night?"

Melena didn't want to answer. The anger she felt was sure to spill over and things would be said that shouldn't be. She faced the wall praying for patience.

Her sister stepped on the bed, climbed over her body, and wedged herself between the wall and Melena's stomach.

"You're on my arm. Get off!"

"Then talk to me."

"Fine, you want to know why I was angry." Melena pushed up on her elbows. "Because you stole two things from me in one night. What were you doing there anyway? It's not even your crowd."

"A girl from my school invited me." Cassi shrugged. "I don't know why you got all weepy about that bracelet. It wasn't even that cute."

Melena pushed back the thought of her birthday gift sinking in the sand. "Where did you meet Dylan?"

"At the party, why?" Her lips pinched tight. "Oh, I get it. You're jealous because I saw him first."

Unbelievable. "Correction, I saw him first at camp, and I'm hardly jealous of *you*." She shoved her sister off and headed for the bathroom.

"Ah, *now*, everything makes sense," Cassi said, trailing her into the small space. "Your tantrum was over a guy."

"Do you mind? I'd like some privacy." She pushed Cassi back and tried to close the door in her face.

The phone rang. Cassi peered over her shoulder. "Sure, take all the time you want. I'll just get that."

"Fine!" Melena slammed the door and turned on the faucet.

"Oh, hi, *Dylan*," Cassi said real loud, obviously for Melena's benefit.

Whatever. Melena rolled her eyes and sat down on the edge of the tub. "Dear Lord, I know this is an awkward place for a conference, but I'm hurting and need your help. I know I promised to be more patient with my sister while I was at camp, but do you see what I have to put up with?" She snatched the towel by the mirror and sighed. "God, I really liked him." Her eyes filled with tears. *I really did.*

****

"Is Melena home?" Dylan asked.

Cassi pouted. "Uh, no. Did you need something? Maybe I can help?"

"No, that's okay."

"I had a really fun time last night. I'm so sorry you had to witness the sparks between my sister and me."

"No big deal. Do you know when she'll return?"

She frowned. Dylan was hot and Cassi wanted him, but from the beginning, it was obvious he liked her sister. All night, he had drilled her about Melena. *What is Melena's favorite perfume? Where does Melena like to go? Would Melena expect a limo to the banquet? Melena, Melena, Melena. Yuck!* It made her sick. Cassi did everything she could to change the subject, but he wouldn't relent. No matter, she never backed down from a challenge. In fact, it would be more fun this way.

She stepped in the hall and glanced at the bathroom door. Still closed. "No, but how would you like to go to the movies with me tonight?"

"Uh, I don't think so."

"My sister could come." She rolled her eyes. Of

course, that would never happen. Cassi would just show up stag with an excuse.

"No, really, thanks. I have loads of unpacking to do. Maybe some other time."

"I could come over to help you unpack. Then maybe you'd be free to go out afterward." *Mellow. You're going to scare him off.*

"No, I don't think so. Just tell your sister I called. Okay?" The line went dead.

This is going to be harder than I thought. She pressed off and held the phone to her side. The bathroom door opened and Melena eyed her.

Cassi sneered. *I'm going to win, Melena. I always do. Deal with it.*

****

Melena shut the door to her room and paced the carpet, while combing her hair. *Why did he call Cassi, and what did he say to make her upset? What happened to Dylan and me? He didn't even look for me at the party.* She collapsed face up on her bed and sighed. *Okay, so he said hi, but only after he flirted with my sister all night.* She chewed her lip. *I need to talk to April.* She walked down to the living room phone and dialed her best friend.

"April, is that you?" Melena said to the faint voice on the other line.

"Yeah." She croaked, then yawned. "What's up?"

"I'm sorry for waking you, but I really need to talk."

"You sound upset."

"I am." Melena folded to the couch. "Things are bad, and I need my best friend."

"Give me a few minutes. I'll catch a ride from my

brother when he leaves for work."

"Thanks." Melena hung up, relieved. April didn't really need to wait for a ride. They'd lived a block away from each other since they were kids. *What sane person would walk, if they had access to a ride?*

Cassi barreled down the stairs and out the front door, without a word.

"Good riddance." Melena flipped on the TV and scoured the digital highway for something worth watching. Nothing but sappy romances and dysfunctional families. *I have enough of my own drama. I don't need to watch it.* She snapped it off and flopped backward on the couch. Dylan's face from the night before stared into her mind's eye. She imagined him walking back to his car hurt and mad. Melena hit the couch with her fist and rolled over. Why'd she have to let her anger destroy everything all the time? *Lord, I want freedom from this drama.* Her eyes welled with fresh tears. She allowed them to fall.

By the time April finally arrived, Melena was a mess.

"What happened?" April placed her purse and cell phone on the glass coffee table and met her friend on the couch.

Melena poured out the last twenty-four hours, gasping to catch her breath. Her heart weighed heavy and her mind seemed lost. The intense crying plugged her nose and throat. Her chest heaved, wracked with sobs.

"Melena, calm down, or you're going to hyperventilate." April rubbed her back, visibly inhaling and exhaling. "Come on, breathe with me."

Melena mimicked her friend and her breathing

began to slow.

"There's no way you and Cassi are from the same gene pool," April said through gritted teeth. "And, there's no way Dylan would choose her over you. She's what, fourteen? And he's got to be nineteen or twenty, right?"

"She turns fifteen in September and I think he's nineteen."

"Jailbait. There's no way your dad will go for that."

Melena blew and wiped her nose. "Yeah, but my mom won't care. She never does. That's why Cassi is so spoiled." She pulled her legs up and placed her chin on her knees. "I really messed up last night. I acted like a raving lunatic."

"I wouldn't really worry about it, Mel." April walked in the kitchen and returned with fresh tissue and draped it over Melena's knee. "He doesn't want your *baby* sister. He's a man, for goodness sake."

"He probably doesn't know her age because she can pull off eighteen, easy."

"Oh, I'll tell him." April scooted forward and retrieved her cell phone.

"No," Melena shrieked and knocked it out of her hand. "Who are you calling?"

"I'm calling Chad to get Dylan's number. Somebody needs to tell him what a fool he's being." April patted under the couch. "Don't do that again. I can't afford a new phone." She slid onto her knees and leaned over. Groaning, she pressed her cheek to the floor. Finally, she found her phone and got back up in a huff.

"You can't call him, April."

"I will, if you don't stop feeling sorry for yourself. I can't stand it."

Melena stared at the purple cell in April's hand. She knew her friend would get his number and not be afraid to dial it. At the risk of being humiliated even worse, she had to buck up. April would see to it. "Fine, I'll stop. For now."

"Good. Now, why don't we go to the Circle K, grab a gallon of ice cream, then come back here, and devour it? We can veg out to an old John Hughes movies."

Melena checked the time on her phone. "It's not even eight in the morning."

"Milk is a breakfast food and ice cream has milk in it." April grinned.

Melena forced a smile. "Okay. Anything but that gross Spumoni you made me eat last time."

"You've got it."

"*And,* my favorite movie—*Pretty in Pink.*"

"Deal." April held out her hand and Melena took it.

After a ten-minute trip to the store, they were ready. April searched online to order the movie, while Melena prepared their ice cream.

"How about *Pretty in Pink* and *While You Were Sleeping*?" April said.

"*While You Were Sleeping* isn't a John Hughes film."

April shrugged. "No, but it's a great chick flick."

"No argument there." She handed April a spoon and a gallon of Cookie Dough.

April's eyes darted back and forth around the living room. "Is it okay to eat in here?"

Melena glanced at the black and white pictures of

her mother, the white carpet, matching couch, and crystal ornaments. "Yep."

"Won't your mom go ballistic?"

Melena pulled off the top of her Rocky Road, scooped up a marshmallow, popped it to her mouth, and smirked. "Yep."

April shook her head and folded to the carpet. "Okay. It's your funeral."

Melena stared at the screen devouring the romantic turmoil of Molly Ringwald's character and finding elation at the final kiss. Melena sighed. *Girl meets boy. Girl loses boy.* A slow smile crept across her face. *Girl gets boy back.*

April selected and ordered the next movie and then lay back down. However, halfway through the second movie, she leapt off the couch. "Oh no, I have to be at work in a few minutes."

"Really? Now? We haven't got to the good part."

"I know, but I promised Sonya I'd cover her shift while she had her sonogram done. It's only for a couple of hours."

Melena thought of their waif Pilipino friend with a swollen torso. "I can't believe she's married, let alone having a baby."

"Pretty soon, all our friends will be off doing the family thing." April placed her spoon on the table and hugged Melena's neck. "Tell me you're going to be okay so I don't accidentally put caffeinated coffee in someone's decaffeinated drink." She laughed, twirling her finger as she said, "Some poor, old guy starts doing wheelies in his wheelchair."

Melena laughed. "Yeah, I'll be okay."

"Promise?"

She nodded and turned off the TV monitor.

"Good, then I'll see you around five." April grabbed her purse and left.

The sudden silence pounded in Melena's head as she stared at the closed door. The emptiness of the white room was overwhelming. As kids, they weren't allowed to play anywhere but outside, for fear they'd mess up the house. *How could anyone feel peace in this place? It's like living in an operating room.*

"Oh, hello, sweetheart. I didn't expect you to be in here." Melena turned around. Her mother's petite frame looked striking in a red suit. Her black hair was pulled into a neat bun and besides a few crows' feet, her skin looked flawless as usual. Melena had always admired the way her mother looked, but that was where the admiration ended. It wasn't that she didn't love her. Of course she did, but her mother was cold and meticulous. Image and posture were more important than hugs and intimacy.

"Honey, is something wrong?" her mother asked over the top of her compact mirror. "I asked you if you enjoyed the party."

Melena blinked. "Enjoyed the party? Um, I don't really want to talk about it." She rose and snatched up the ice cream cartons and spoons. "When did you get home?"

"A few minutes ago." Her mom stared at the contents in Melena's hands for a moment and then replied, "Have you seen your sister this morning? I didn't hear her come in last night."

Melena grimaced. "Yeah, I saw her."

"What a relief." She snapped her compact closed and shoved it in her handbag. "Brian should be home this evening from his trip. Did you want to eat with us?"

"Uh, I can't." Melena stepped back. "I have plans to go out with some friends up north tonight."

Her mother forced a pout. "That's too bad. Maybe another time then."

"Yeah, sure. Well, Mom, I have tons to do. So, I should probably get going." She sidestepped to the kitchen.

"Come give your mother a kiss first, will you? I hardly see you these days." She tilted her cheek.

Melena leaned and kissed her. *Always so formal.* Her mother pretended to care and be a mom, but she had yet to fool Melena. It wasn't a job she was cut out to do. Four times she had tried and four times she had failed.

"Bye, Mom."

"Melena?"

"Yes, Mom?"

Her mother swayed her eyes to the white couch. "Please don't eat outside the kitchen again."

Melena bit her lip. "Yes, Mom."

"Thank you." She dipped her head, picked up the morning paper from the entryway, and then walked toward the master suite.

Melena went in the kitchen, dropped the spoons in the sink, and shoved the ice cream in the freezer. *Oh, it was so worth it.* She laughed to herself.

The front door opened.

Melena peeked around the wall. *Great, the black plague has returned.* She flipped back into the kitchen, secretly praying Cassi wasn't hungry. Melena wasn't in the mood for another encounter with the beast.

"Cassi, I need to see you for a moment," her mom said.

"Just a minute, Mom. I have something to take care of." Her feet pounded on the stairs, then her bedroom door slammed shut.

Melena stepped out, darting her eyes to make sure the coast was clear, and rushed the stairs. The phone rang and she froze.

Her mother answered on the first ring. "Hello? Oh, yes, hold on a minute. Melena..."

Her heart thumped like a mad jackrabbit as she ran to the living room extension. She held her hand over the mouthpiece and yelled, "I've got it!" Then placed the phone to her ear. "Hello?"

"Melena or Cassi?"

"Dylan?" Melena frowned. "Who were you looking for?" *Good girl, Melena, answer a question, with a question.*

"I'm guessing Melena, right?" He laughed. "I was looking for you, of course."

Of course. She smiled.

"I really need to get your cell number." He laughed. "Hey, I was wondering if you..."

At the same time, Melena began, "Look about last night..."

They both laughed.

"You first," he said.

"I'm really sorry about last night. I know I was kind of a jerk."

"No, I get it. My older brother and I have had a few fights in our time. Only when *we're* done, there's blood."

"Really?"

He laughed. "Okay, maybe I'm exaggerating a bit. It's more like bruises and broken bones."

She giggled. "I didn't know you had a brother."

"Half-brother. My dad was married once before when he was real young."

"Oh, are you…"

Cassi's voice abruptly came on the line. "Dylan, how are you?"

"Uh, fine…"

"Cassi, get off the line!" Melena stared up the stairs.

"Did you consider our date yet?"

Unbelievable. Heat rushed down Melena's neck. "Cassi, the phone is for me."

Dylan cleared his throat. "I was planning to ask *Melena* out tonight."

"You were?" Melena smiled.

"I'm sure she would like that, but she can't go. Can you, Melena?"

"Sure I can."

"No, you can't. It's Monday. You always go to the mall with your friends on Mondays, am I right? After all, they're coming all the way down from the O.C. to be with you. You wouldn't want to disappoint them."

Why does the little creep know my schedule? Anger boiled in Melena's skull. *Is it life in prison if I murder Cassi for pushing me too far?* Plotting the flowers for her sister's funeral, she relented.

"Yeah, I am supposed to…"

"*See*, so, how about it, Dylan?"

There was a long pause. *What's taking him so long to reply? Just say no. Simple. N-O.*

"Um, I guess…"

Melena's heart sank. She blinked back the tears and willed her voice not to crack. "Okay, well, you two have fun." Numb, Melena set the receiver back in its cradle, walked back to her room, and threw herself on the bed face first. Maybe he really did like her sister. A memory of them together slapped her. *Fine! He can have her.* Melena wasn't strong like April or forward like Cassi. She didn't have the will to fight when it came to guys. Hot tears saturated her pillow. She flipped over and stared out the open window. The trees waved in the lazy afternoon sun. A group of kids splashed in a pool somewhere nearby, a dog barked at someone mowing a lawn, and a steady rhythm of traffic could be heard in the distance. The morning sounds usually soothed her, but today they sounded deafening.

"What do I do, Lord?" she whispered. "I just don't know how to deal with this pain. I'm not my sister. I can't win against her." Melena relaxed against her pillow and continued to pray silently. The sleepless night, early rise, and assault of emotion overtook her and she drifted to sleep.

Chapter Eight

Dylan blinked, confused. Melena had hung up before he could finish his sentence. He was about to say, "I guess we'll have to do it another time."

"So, it looks like it's just you and me, Dylan."

He rolled his eyes. "You know what, Cassi. I forgot I have other plans. I'll talk to you later, okay?"

Quickly, he hit the red button on his cell phone and jammed it in his pocket. Bass and drums thumped from the room above his head. The increase in his sister's music jarred him. *I need to get out of here.* He glanced through the window at his dirty Jeep. *As good a time as any.*

He patted his pocket for keys. It jingled. *Good.* He pushed the screen door and walked into the yard. *What was going through Melena's head anyway? Does she like me or not?* That was the second time she'd blown him off in two days. He crossed to his vehicle and hopped in. As he pulled out into traffic, he flipped open his cell and dialed.

Chad answered on the first ring. "Chad, here."

"Hey, man. You got plans tonight?"

"I thought about going surfing with Nate, but I heard the current is gnarly. One of the guys got hurt this morning."

"Really?"

"Yeah, he hit the rocks pretty hard. They

medevac'd him to Mercy."

"Anyone I know?"

"Nah." Chad coughed, then said, "So, what'd you have planned?"

"I'm thinking about hanging at the mall."

"The mall?"

Dylan smiled. He could imagine Chad's scrunched up face. His friend didn't do much that didn't involve water or music. Well, and girls.

Dylan stopped at a red light and glanced in his rearview mirror. "April and Melena are going to be there."

"Those two hot birds. Okay, yeah, I'm game."

That did it. "I just need you to do me a favor first." The light turned green and Dylan pulled into the carwash lot.

"What's that?"

Dylan exhaled. "I need you to call April incognito and find out which mall."

****

"Wake up, Melena." April's voice came through a fog. "Wake up, will you?"

Melena groaned. "I'm up already."

"Why are you sleeping?" April flopped down on the bed causing the mattress to jiggle. "You're not even ready to go."

"I fell asleep."

"I can see that." April grinned. "Guess who called me to find out what mall we are going to?"

Melena pushed her back up to her headboard and peeked through her lids. "Who?"

"Chad. He tried to act so nonchalant, but I could tell he was fishing. So hurry up, we have got to get there right away." She hit Melena's thigh, then jumped up, and tossed her a pair of jean shorts. "Besides Kelly's waiting."

"Wait, slow down." Melena pulled off her sweats and replaced them with the shorts. "Dylan won't be with him. He's supposed to be going to the movies with Cassi tonight."

"No, he's not. Chad said he and Dylan were hanging out tonight. So, come on." She delved through the dresser drawer and held up a red and black floral top. "This always looks good on you."

"Dylan and Chad are at the mall?"

April frowned. "Yes, they will be. Why isn't this computing with you?"

"Fine, but I don't know if I want to meet up with Dylan."

April stopped rummaging and faced her open-mouthed. "What? Don't be dumb."

Melena's eyes narrowed. "I'm not dumb. I'm just cautious."

"You're always cautious and look where it's got you."

"Um, with an undamaged heart."

April crossed her arms and stared her in the eye. "That's not true. How about Enrique?"

Melena shifted her gaze to the beige carpet. "What about him?"

"You've shed many tears over that guy and haven't taken a chance once." She walked over and took Melena's hand. "Dylan likes you, Mel."

"You should have seen them at the party." The horrid vision of Dylan talking in Cassi's ear flashed through her mind. "I'm not sure I can take that again."

"He's a nice guy and you *know* your sister. I promise it was Cassi's doing." April tossed her the top. "Now come on. Snap out of it and let's get going."

Melena snatched the shirt and ran in the bathroom. Her adrenaline kicked in, waking her up and filling her with excitement. She finished getting dressed, applied some makeup, and ran a brush through her hair. Turning her face side-to-side, she said, "Why can't I look like my sister?"

"Because God blessed you with good looks." April stepped in the doorway and smirked. "Come on."

Melena laughed. "Okay, let's go."

*****

From the parking lot, Melena spotted her friends hanging out at the two-story mall entrance. Keith and Shawn slouched against a cement wall, laughing with Tiffany and Kelly.

Melena frowned. "If I knew we were inviting guys tonight, I could have asked Dylan to come in the first place."

"Hmm?" April followed her gaze. "Well, he's going to be here anyway. So, no big-D."

"Are we meeting them somewhere?"

April shook her head. "I told you, Chad was fishing. So, Dylan's in the right stream, we just have to put out the right bait." She looked Melena over. "And honey, you've got it."

Melena laughed. "You're ridiculous. Come on."

As they weeded through cars, a question gnawed at Melena. *Why isn't Dylan with my sister? He did ask for me. But maybe I'm just his tool to get close to Cassi.* Melena closed her eyes and inhaled. Though her thoughts were absurd, she couldn't stop feeding them.

The image of Dylan and Cassi sitting close at the party infuriated her. By the time they reached the front of the mall, she was on the verge of tears.

"Hi, April. Hi, Mel." Kelly swung her arms out in front of her. "Isn't it a beautiful night? I just love a full moon." The petite redhead was more cheerful than Barney at a birthday party. She always wore a smile and spewed sunshine. Her red hair, fair skin, and freckles complimented her personality. Everyone jokingly called her "Annie."

Melena forced a grin. "Hey."

"What's wrong?" Good ole' Keith, always to the rescue. Kelly's boyfriend was also her brother Nick's best friend. He'd been hanging out with the Harrison family for years.

"Nothing, I'm just tired," Melena said.

"Well, let's get some caffeine and sugar at the bakery then." He looped his arm in hers, draped his other arm around Kelly, and escorted them through the open doorway.

"I love caffeine and sugar." Kelly beamed.

Keith kissed the top of her head and whispered, "And I love you."

April caught Melena's eye and smiled.

Melena bit her lip and turned away.

"Hey, April," Shawn said. "Do you think you can get us a discount today?"

She shook her head. "No, my boss isn't on and Missy hates me."

"Bummer."

They went up the escalator and walked to their favorite bakery. Kelly talked a mile a minute, but Melena missed most of what she said. Her thoughts were far from her group of friends. Maybe she should have gone with Dylan. Her friends would understand. She mentally whacked herself upside the head. Everyone, except Melena, piled inside the bakery to get in line. Instead, she stopped at the door. Nausea swept through her.

Cassi sat a few tables from the front, enrapt in a conversation with a half-dozen guys. They seemed intrigued with a story that was probably an exaggeration too cute too resist.

April glanced back at Melena and joined her in the doorway. "What's wrong?"

"Great." Melena gaped through the bakery window. "What's she doing here?"

April sighed. "Dylan stood her up and she probably had nothing else to do."

"With my luck, she's meeting him here."

"Don't be silly. I already told you, he isn't going out with her."

"Maybe you're wrong. Maybe she's meeting him at the movies later. It's hopeless. Let's just go home."

April's eyes blazed. She snatched Melena's sleeve and pulled her around the corner. "How are you and I even friends?" She clutched Melena's shoulders and looked at her with narrowed eyes. "Why do you let your sister walk all over you? She hasn't won unless you let her. Don't you dare give her the satisfaction." April breathed out and her expression softened. "Dylan likes you, Mel. I'm sure of it."

Melena heard April's words, but they were far from reassuring where Cassi was concerned. The girl was ruthless and always finagled her way, leaving Melena in her wake. An overwhelming sense of doom flooded her heart. She wanted to quit. To admit defeat, return home, and end her evening crying into a pillow. But one glance at April and she knew that wasn't going to happen. April's jaw was tight, her eyes incensed. Her friend was ready for a fight. If Melena didn't give her the response she wanted, she'd be livid.

"Okay." Melena half-grinned. "I'm sorry."

April wrapped an arm around her and squeezed. "Now, let's go inside and get a latte. A little caffeine rush and we'll go find *your* boyfriend, okay?"

Over April's shoulder, Melena spotted Dylan and Chad walking into a video arcade. Her heart leapt. "They're here." She pointed.

April twisted, then grabbed her wrist. "Come on."

They turned to go, but smacked into Cassi, who blocked their path, arms crossed and a smirk on her face. "What are you doing here?" Her sister looked her up and down with a curled lip and flared nostrils. "Are you following me?"

"Give me a break. You *knew* I was going to be here tonight."

She flung her hair over her shoulder and sniffed. "Must have slipped my mind."

"Right," Melena sneered.

April rolled her eyes. "So, where's Dylan?"

"He forgot he had other plans." Cassi sniggered, "But don't you worry, sis, he gave me a rain check."

"Whatever." April pushed past her. "Let's go, Mel."

"Later." Melena stepped around her sister and followed her friend across the aisle into the dark arcade. The room buzzed with flashing lights, loud beeps, and laughter. It took a second for her eyes to adjust.

April did a one-eighty around the room. "Are you sure they came in here?"

Melena smiled. "Positive. There's Chad." She walked up behind him and tapped his arm. "Hey, Chad."

He made a quick glance from the game over his shoulder. "Hey, Melena. Dylan's been looking everywhere for you."

April elbowed Melena's ribs.

Chad frantically punched a button with one hand and maneuvered a joystick with the other. On the screen, an asteroid flew in from the side and destroyed his ship. "Drat!" He shook his head and turned from the game. "So, ladies, looking good, per usual."

They giggled.

"Where's Dylan?" Melena said.

Chad peered beyond them.

Melena spun around.

Dylan stood inches from her with a huge grin. "Well, look who we have here."

Her cheeks burned. "Hi, Dylan."

"You're a hard girl to find."

"Aren't you supposed to be on a date with Cassi?" she said.

He snorted. "That wasn't my idea." Dylan stepped behind Chad and her and wrapped his hands around both of their shoulders. "I mean, there I was, talking to this great girl. Her sister gets on the line and insists I take her out. I'm never one to be rude, but…" He let go and turned to her. "I told her I forgot I had other plans."

April crossed her arms and leaned in at the waist. "Did you know she's at the mall?"

Chad laughed. "Yeah, we've been dodging her all

73

night."

"It hasn't been easy." Dylan leaned against the game with a lazy smile. "Why don't we get out of this noisy arcade and go see that movie?"

Melena grinned. "I'd love that."

He took her hand and nodded for Chad and April to follow. Dylan leaned over and whispered, "April won't mind, will she?"

Melena peered over at her friend. The huge smile plastered on her face answered the question. "No, I'm pretty sure she'll be fine." She met April's gaze. "We should probably let Kelly know what we're doing."

April nodded. "Let's go by the bakery and we'll introduce you."

The two couples walked across the aisle and into the bakery. The room smelt of fresh baked bread and roasted coffee. Melena weaved her way around tables to her friends, who sat in the back corner.

"Where did you go?" Keith asked.

Melena glanced over her shoulder. Chad stood at the counter ordering a drink and Dylan watched her with a lazy smile. "Remember that guy I mentioned?"

Kelly nodded.

"That's him."

Her friends all redirected their gaze to Dylan. He smiled and waved.

Melena flicked her head, indicating he should join them. "Dylan, these are my good friends—Kelly, Keith, Shawn, and Tiffany."

"Hey," Dylan said, looking from face to face. "Nice to meet you."

"Um, Kelly, can I talk to you for a moment?"

She pushed out from under the table and walked a

few feet away, out of earshot. Melena stepped to her. "Would you be okay if April and I didn't stay?"

Kelly peeked around Melena at Dylan, then back to her. "Yeah, I can see why you'd want to ditch me."

"I know you all came down here to be with me."

She shrugged. "Tiffany is here. I haven't seen her since she moved. Plus Keith came, so, it's cool."

"You know, you could come to the movies with us."

"Nah, that's okay. I think we're going to just hang here for a while and catch up." She smiled. "You go ahead, but I'll want details later."

"Thanks, Kel." Melena hugged her. "I'll call you later this week. Next Monday, maybe April and I can go up to see you this time."

"Okay." Kelly waved and went back to her group.

Melena looked at Dylan and smiled. "Ready?"

"Yep."

As they walked through the mall, Dylan and Chad stopped several times to ogle technical gadgets and paintball guns. Melena and April ran ahead and scoped out booths filled with jewelry or windows with cute clothes. Of course, Melena knew nothing about fashion. It was just more fun than standing behind the guys, waiting for them to finish drooling over the electronics.

When they reached the theater at the end of the mall, Dylan turned to her. "So, what looks good?"

Melena studied the marquee. The selections were scary, disgusting, or too romantic for a first date. "Not much out right now, huh?"

"Any chance you're hungry?" Dylan said.

Her stomach had been growling since the moment she met him in the arcade, but she still lacked an appetite. Food looked repulsive no matter how hungry she was. *Can I actually eat in his presence?* "A little."

"You guys see anything you want to watch?" Dylan asked.

"Not really," Chad said.

"Want to eat instead?" Dylan pointed at the Flying Dragon across from the theater. "I could go for some fried wontons."

"I'm game," April said, folding a piece of chewed gum back in its wrapper.

Chinese food? Nasty. It wasn't that Melena didn't love Chinese, because she did. But with her current condition, i.e. love sickness, she couldn't imagine it. However, she was a coward. Always afraid to say anything that might upset someone. It was her downfall. "Sounds great." *Now smile and look like you mean it.* She grinned.

"Then it's settled." He squeezed her hand and guided her through the gold entryway. Inside, the red room was packed with wall-to-wall people feasting on Chinese gourmet. The smell of cooked vegetables and oil permeated the air. An Asian woman in a kimono stepped forward and gave a slight nod. "How many?"

Chad peered down the line, apparently counting bodies. "Four," he said.

"This way." The lady snatched four large, red menus from the shelf and glided through the busy room to a booth in the back corner. "Someone be right with you." She nodded, turned, and returned to her post.

Chad and April scooted around the semi-circular booth and stopped in the middle.

Dylan shook his head. "Keep moving."

Chad smiled and scooted the rest of the way, to the

end.

Melena climbed in and Dylan settled next to her. "Why don't we each order a different thing and share?" he said.

"Orange chicken," April said, sliding her menu back to the end of the table. "I'm easy."

"Great choice, darlin'." Chad winked and turned back to the menu. He studied it for a second, then slapped it down. "Beef lo mein for me." He pretended to cock a cowboy hat and chew a piece straw, while talking in a southern accent. "I'm a meat and potato kind of guy. Gotta have me some cow."

April laughed. "A cowboy from Del Mar."

"Hey, they got lots of horses in them thar hills."

She shook her head and looked at Melena. "What are you getting, Mel?"

Melena stared at the menu. The words blurred. Nothing looked good. Maybe soup. "Wonton Soup."

"I think that comes with the meal. Pick something else," she said.

Melena stuffed her face back in the menu. *Something else. Yeah, okay.* "Egg rolls then."

"Wonton soup and egg rolls for the little lady it is."

April playfully smacked Chad's arm. "Enough cowboy, or we're going to toss you out with the pigs."

"Harsh."

Melena watched Chad and April flirt with each other. Chad wore a black T-shirt and a leather bracelet, and his hair was scooped to the middle like a fohawk. April had on a red and black striped tee along with some red lipstick and a bit too much pomade, because her cropped cut was spiked more than usual. *They look like Sid and Nancy. Well, minus the body piercings and profanity.* Melena lifted her hand to hide her grin. She shifted her gaze to the restaurant full of people. Couples sat quietly around the room, talking, eating, and having a good time. Her eyes ended at Dylan. He studied his menu, oblivious to her stare. He looked great in the blue striped polo. His face had a slight burn to his tan, probably from surfing in the early morning fog, and a shell necklace clutched his neck. *He's here with me. Who would have thought I would be coupled up, too?*

Dylan closed his menu and placed it on top of the others. "I'm voting for shrimp fried rice."

"Good call," Chad said.

"You think everything is good." April grinned.

He winked. "Yes, I do."

The waitress came over and took their order. Within ten minutes or so, she returned with enormous portions of Chinese cuisine.

Melena's stomach voiced its complaint. It seemed to growl, *don't even think about it.* "That's a lot of food."

"Yes, and we'll eat it all." Chad rubbed his hands together, then reached for a glass bowl filled with noodles and vegetables.

Melena barely filled her plate. She hated to come off like one of those girls who ate like a bird, but she couldn't help it. Dylan made her nervous.

Dylan sipped his tea, then asked, "So, how do you two know each other? Isn't April still in high school?"

April tilted her head to the side. "Don't make it sound like a bad thing."

"I'm not. Just curious." He winked at Melena.

Man, he's gorgeous. He's staring at me. He's cute and he's actually here, with me! She blinked, trying to

78

block out the wave of butterflies that took flight. "Um, we grew up playing together. April lives about ten houses down from my mom."

"We were inseparable until her dad moved to Orange County a few years ago." April peeled off the skin of an egg roll and popped it in her mouth.

"Yeah, the divorce was hard for a lot of reasons." Melena toyed with a noodle on her plate. "I still come down for a lot of the church events, and she's good friends with some of my friends from school."

April shrugged. "Yeah, and the drive isn't too bad. About an hour, if there isn't any traffic."

"I'll have to remember that." Dylan touched Melena's elbow with the back of his hand.

Volcanic energy shot through her body. She pretended fascination with the silverware. No doubt her cheeks were crimson.

"So, when do you ladies need to be home?" Chad asked with a Cheshire grin.

****

After dinner, they decided to take a walk at the La Jolla Coves. Melena had always loved the coves that walled the ocean. The coves had little sand and when the tide was low, all sorts of wildlife were left behind.

As they strolled along the rocky path, the ocean spray shot at least forty-feet high mere yards away. The luminous moon cast shadows from the cliffs behind them and a soft wind sent the smell of salt and sea life through the air. Chad and April stepped out of the rocks and went by the ocean shore.

Dylan assisted Melena over a large rock, then rested against another with crossed arms.

"I love this place. Your mom is so lucky to work

here." She pushed herself up on the edge of the rock, letting her legs dangle over the side. In the distance, the lull of the waves could be heard in the dark. Silhouetted by the moonlight, April and Chad wandered along the beach about twenty feet away, laughing.

April, what are you doing? She had a boyfriend. *Always the flirt. Maybe I should tell Dylan...* Melena glanced at him.

His eyes locked with hers.

Her heart raced, electrical currents shot up her spine. Her head swam. His lips were moist and inviting, but she feared his approach.

Dylan stepped forward and held her hands to his chest. Her heart accelerated. He leaned in and his lips met hers. Soft and warm. *Is this really happening?*

He slowly pulled back and smiled. His eyes were gentle. "You okay? You're trembling."

Was she? She didn't notice. "I'm great."

He smiled, then relaxed on the rock next to her. "So, I tried to siphon information out of your sister the other day, but she wouldn't give up much."

The mention of Cassi caused a ripple in the magic. Melena forced a grin. "What kind of information?"

"Oh, I don't know." He let go of her hand and wrapped his arm around her shoulders. "What kind of music you listen to? Your favorite flower? Favorite food? You know, that kind of stuff."

Melena smiled. "The four-one-one."

"Exactly."

She thought about that for a moment. Her mind was a bit fuzzy with the realization that Dylan was so close. So warm. "I like alternative and retro fifties through the eighties."

"Favorite bands?"

"Um… Switchfoot…" The rock she sat on started to hurt underneath her. She shifted a bit. "…Bon Jovi, the Police, U2, Men at Work." She threw her hands in the air. "There's so many. I don't even know how to list them all. What about you?"

"My favorite of all time would have to be…" He scratched his chin. "Sandy Patty. Without a doubt."

Melena laughed. "What? No way."

He smirked. "What's wrong with that?"

"Sandy Patty? Please. My grandmother listens to her."

He tickled her side and she scrambled to get away. He held her hands against him and pulled her in. His lips met hers.

"Are you guys ready to go?" Chad yelled.

Dylan pulled back, but kept his gaze fixed on Melena's. "It's early."

"Curfew for us minors is midnight," April said and popped a bubble loud enough for them to hear over the waves.

"Well, I guess that means I can stay." He winked and Melena smiled.

"I can't," April said.

"You're not a minor," Chad said. "You're eighteen."

"Yeah, tell my mom that."

Melena stood and wiped at her pants. "April's mom has been in a mood lately. We'd better go."

Dylan wrapped his arm around Melena's waist and led her down to the sand. They walked through the supple earth to his Jeep. Chad and April piled in back.

Melena moved to climb in, too, but Dylan blocked

her with his arm. "Wait."

She searched his eyes. "Is everything okay?"

He touched her chin and placed his lips to hers.

Fire raced down her neck and into every joint. Her heart hammered in her chest. *Just breathe.*

"Can I drive you home?" he whispered.

"Sure." Her head whirled. "I mean, wait." She giggled. "My car is back at the mall."

He kissed the back of her hand. "Can April drive it?"

She smiled. "Sure."

Dylan leaned over the Jeep's rail. "Can we drop the two of you off at the mall? You two could take Melena's car."

Chad beamed. "Another ten minutes alone with this hot chick. Absolutely."

April laughed. "Where do you live, Chad?"

"Del Mar Heights Road."

"That's close." She turned back to Dylan. "Yeah, that's fine."

"Boy, it's tight back here," Chad said, squeezing up against April. "Though I'm not complaining." He smiled.

April grinned and grabbed onto the bar next to her head.

About fifteen minutes later, they left Chad and April at Melena's car. "Thanks, April. See you tomorrow."

"Bye, Mel," then mouthed, "Call me."

Melena nodded, smiled, then shut the door, and re-buckled her seatbelt. "They really hit it off, didn't they?"

"So did we." He kissed her again.

He pulled back and turned the key in the engine. It roared to life. They pulled out of the mall and onto the surface street. She held her hair, as the wind whipped at her face and took a deep breath.

"Are you cold?" he yelled, adjusting the heater vents. "Jeeps aren't the warmest cars in the world."

She shook her head. "Nah, I'm fine."

"You should put your number in my phone," he stated, handing it to her.

She smiled and punched in the numbers. "I'm not sure why we didn't do that to begin with."

He reached out and took her hand.

She enjoyed the ride back to her house. Without the top up, the wind was too loud for conversation, so she didn't have to worry about talking and could just enjoy the company. The stars were bright, the moon full, and the air warm—the perfect San Diego summer night. She closed her eyes for a moment and listened to the buzz of the engine and cars whizzing by. She touched her lips and remembered his kiss.

Dylan stared ahead, a slight grin on his face.

Melena smiled and looked back at the road. She sensed him turn and look at her. For fear of red cheeks, she didn't return his gaze.

He pulled in front of her brown two-story house. Melena looked out the window and sighed. He came around to let her out. She took his hand and let him escort her to the door. At the end of the walkway, he turned to face her. "I had a good time."

She smiled. "Me, too. One question though?"

"What's that?" He stepped closer to her and wrapped his arms around her waist.

"Who really is your favorite band?"

He stood close enough she could feel his breath on her skin. "Probably U2."

"We have that in common." She smiled, his lips millimeters from hers.

"Yeah." He brushed his lips to hers.

A car door slammed in the driveway.

Dylan pulled back and glanced over.

Cassi.

He looked back at Melena and winked. "Good night." He kissed her lightly on the forehead and walked away.

Melena wished she had a camera ready. Bug-eyed, open-mouthed, the look on her sister's face was golden.

"What's he doing here?" Cassi said, through clenched teeth.

"Walking me to the door."

"I can see that! I mean, what were you doing with *my* guy?"

"Your guy? Hmm?" Melena lifted an eyebrow and spun around to unlock the door. "He was never *your* guy. He was *my* guy that you *tried* to hone in on." Melena pushed the door open and stepped inside. "Besides, he never had any interest in you…he's just too nice to say so."

"I hate you."

Melena laughed and skipped up the stairs. She could hear Cassi's tantrum, but tonight, she didn't care. Safe inside her room, Melena collapsed on the bed and squealed. The taste of saltwater still lingered on her lips and the smell of his cologne on her clothes. Her stomach flipped as he filled her thoughts. *Now I'll never get to sleep.*

Chapter Nine

The next morning, Dylan sat at the kitchen table twirling his cell phone, a grin plastered on his face. He loved the way Melena wore her hair. Always down, soft around her shoulders. His other girlfriend always had hers in a ponytail. He tried to get her to wear it down, but she never would.

Get Renee out of your head. You're with Melena now. He smiled again, then slid the screen on his phone, and exhaled.

His sister flew in the room and threw open drawers left and right. Peeking high and low, in search of who knows what.

"Whoa! Slow down, sis." He laughed. "What's the hurry?"

She glanced at him, before sticking her head in another cupboard. "Mom and I are going to Sea World." She pulled out a box of baggies, then continued her mission. "Want to come?"

Dylan considered that for a second. He weighed the two in his mind's scale: seeing Melena again versus walking around staring at a bunch of fish. "Nope, sorry. I have plans." He spun his cell phone again and stood. "Have fun though. Say hi to Shamu for me."

She didn't look up, just squatted to peer into the lower cabinet.

Dylan chuckled and walked back to the den.

Closing the door, he hit Melena's number.

****

In the distance, Melena could hear bells. She didn't want to open her eyes to see their location. Her lids were so heavy from a lack of sleep. The ringing stopped. Her phone lay on the nightstand lit up. She snatched it up and frowned. *Oh no. Dylan had called.* She pushed the voicemail.

"I guess you're still sleeping…" came Dylan's voice. "I was kind of hoping…Chad and I surf early most days. We're usually home by eight. He never showed this morning, so I thought I'd call and see if you were interested in breakfast."

She quickly dialed his number.

"Hello?"

"Sorry, Dylan. I didn't pick up in time. Breakfast sounds great." She glanced down at her sweat shorts and T-shirt. "Um, I just now crawled out of bed. Can you give me a half hour?"

"That's it? I'm impressed."

She smiled. "Yeah, I'm pretty low-maintenance."

"I like that."

She cursed her red cheeks. *Thank goodness we're not Skyping.* "So, I'll see you in thirty minutes."

"Count on it."

"Bye." She set the phone down, turned over, stuffed her face in the pillow, and screamed, "Aah!!!" *Okay, I've got thirty minutes to get cute.* She faced her closet and stared, willing inspiration. Nothing jumped out to her. *Fine. What would April choose?* She walked over to her drawer and withdrew a pair of white shorts and a pink T-shirt with silver letters that read, "Bump, Set, Spike."

It's me. And that's who I'm trying to be. She quickly showered, got dressed, and finished her makeup in record time. She was just slipping on her last tennis shoe when the doorbell rang.

She opened the door and Dylan let out a low whistle. "You look beautiful."

"Thanks." She smiled shyly, then ran her eyes over his clothes. He wore cargo shorts, a black surfer shirt, and Birkenstocks. He smelled of soap and cologne and his spiked hair was still damp. "You look pretty good, too."

"We make one hot couple." He reached for her hand and led her down the driveway. "Where do you want to go?"

She shrugged. "Wherever you want." *Wouldn't want to actually voice my opinion.*

"Where would you and April go?"

"Our House of Pancakes?" *It slipped out. But there it is, the truth. I hope that's okay.* "But we don't have to go there if you don't want to."

He opened the Jeep door and she stepped in. "Our House, it is."

On the ride over, she couldn't help but stare at him. *A nice Christian, he's gorgeous and likes me. Miracles are real.*

They pulled into the lot and he parked. "I've never eaten here before."

She peered out the window at the big red roof. "Really? They've got amazing fruit pancakes."

He walked around and let her out. "Come on. I'm starved."

Inside, the waitress seated them in a booth in back. As Melena thumbed through the menu, the thought occurred to her that she still didn't have an appetite. *I'm going to be skinnier than Laura Flynn Boyle if I don't get over this nervousness.* "I'll just have a yogurt and fruit."

Dylan stared at her a moment and then ordered. "I'll take the He-man Egg Breakfast with pancakes instead of toast. An extra egg, over easy. Bacon only, with country potatoes."

The waitress nodded and walked away.

Melena giggled. "You don't eat much, do you?"

He laughed. "You should talk."

"Actually, I usually have a big appetite." *Please don't blush.* "It's just around you…I'm a bit nervous."

He intertwined his fingers with hers. "I feel the same about you."

Yep, heat rising. Hope you like your woman with rosy cheeks. "Yeah, okay." She laughed. "That's why you ordered the He-man meal."

He puffed out his chest, lifted his chin in the air, and spoke in a deep voice. "Normally, I'd eat two."

She giggled. "Funny."

He let go of her hand, wadded a straw wrapper, and flicked it at her.

She snatched it and tossed it at his face. It missed and flew at the elderly couple behind him.

Dylan bit his lip. "Nice going."

"Whoops." She pretended to hide her embarrassment behind her napkin.

"Never played paper football with your brothers?"

"Guess not." She lowered her paper shelter and took a sip of her water. "So, what did you think of camp?"

"Besides the night hike?" He offered her a coy

smile.

She stared down at the table and grinned. "Yeah, besides that."

He must have enjoyed her embarrassment, because he studied her a prolonged time before answering. "Honestly, I was touched." He poured some creamer in his coffee and grabbed a spoon. "God really moved, you know?"

"Yeah, He was moving. I just wished it would all sink in."

The waitress placed their food in front of them. "Can I get you anything else?"

Dylan surveyed their bounty and shook his head. "No, I think we're good. Thanks." He looked back at Melena as the waitress walked away. "You were saying."

"Ever since my parents divorced, I've really struggled with bitterness. Scott kept talking about giving our issues to God and starting over. But it's so hard." She fingered a strand of her hair and exhaled. "You know what I mean?"

He met her eyes. "Look at who Jesus hung out with. He never looked for perfect people, just people with willing hearts. If you desire to change, He'll bless that."

"Yeah." She wiped the condensation from her cup and sighed. "It would be a lot easier if I could make things right with my sister."

"Speaking of your sister, what's her deal, anyway?"

Melena looked down at her bowl of melon and grapes. *Where do I start?* "It's kind of complicated. We're two totally different people. I like alternative, she likes hip-hop. I wear conservative T-shirts and jeans. She wears revealing name brand whatever. I go to church, she's a heathen. We have nothing in common."

"Except she likes me."

Melena rolled her eyes and laughed. "Seems we agree on one thing."

"Kind of makes it difficult for you."

"Not any more than usual." She pursed her lips, trying to hold back the flood of anxiety that poured out with the mention of Cassi. "Do you think we could talk about something else?"

"Sure." He grabbed a glass pitcher the waitress left and proceeded to drown his pancakes in maple syrup. "Chad and I were talking about the church summer banquet. I want to support Teen Challenge any way I can, so I'm going. How about going with me?"

She tried to swallow the grape she'd just popped in her mouth, but choked instead. Her face warmed as she coughed.

Dylan pushed a glass of water toward her. "Here. Drink this."

She took a sip, wiped at her watery eyes, then croaked, "I'd love to."

He lifted an eyebrow. "Are you okay?"

"Guess you caught me off guard." She took another sip and cleared her throat. "I'm fine, really."

"How about we go to the mall Saturday to pick out outfits?"

"Sure." She beamed.

"Cool." He bit into his pancakes and smiled.

Melena looked down at her yogurt and grimaced. *No way am I going to eat now. You stupid, butterflies.*

Stop doing the cha cha in my stomach. Instead, she smashed cantaloupe and honeydew with her fork until it liquefied.

Dylan didn't seem to notice as he inhaled three eggs, four pancakes, a bunch of bacon, and a mound of hash browns.

If we are what we eat, Dylan, you are a He-man. She grinned.

"What's funny?"

She diverted her gaze back to her bowl. "Nothing."

"I like that you're always smiling."

"I think you told me that before."

He pushed his plate away and placed a twenty on their check. "Then I guess it must not be a lie." He winked. "Are you ready?"

She nodded and slid out of the booth.

He led her back to the car and they climbed in. The parking area was a bit crowded and it took a moment for them to get out of the lot. Finally, he was free to pull out into traffic, but turned the car the wrong way.

She pointed over her shoulder. "My house is the other direction."

He smiled. "You want to go to the beach?"

She looked down at her T-shirt and shorts. "I don't have a bathing suit."

He tugged on the hem of his shirt and smiled. "Me either. How 'bout it? It'll be fun."

More time with him or a day with Cassi. Hmmm? That's a toughie. "Sure. Let's go."

He adjusted his mirror. "So, when you're not running off to the beach with some guy from Florida, what do you do for fun? Do you have a job?"

She laughed. "How could you put those two things

91

together? Work and fun."

"It all depends on what you do."

"Hmm, I guess." She reached in her bag and withdrew her sunglasses. "I'm not working right now. I worked in a bookstore last semester, but took the time off to come to my mom's. I'll apply somewhere once I get back up there." She adjusted her seat belt and looked at him. "As for fun, I drink lots of coffee, try to keep April grounded, and play volleyball."

"Volleyball, huh?"

"I played all four years of high school and almost received a scholarship. But that's a whole other issue." She batted at the air. "Last season, I played with an indoor club."

"Are you any good?" He smirked.

She gave him a dirty look and he laughed. "Last year, I played in Division B. This year, I am hoping for Division A."

"And I'm assuming A is better?"

"Yes."

He pulled off at the exit to the beach and reached to turn down the air conditioning. "Are you cold?"

She was freezing. But of course didn't say so. "I'm fine." She shifted in her seat to face him. "Division B is like second string, only they play each other. A is the higher division."

"And that's what you want?"

"Yeah. I have this dream to be a Division A Spiker."

"Spiker?"

"I went to this game once with my brother. It was the best game I'd ever seen. The Spikers were amazing." She glanced at the road in reflective thought.

"It was after that game I knew I wanted to play volleyball. They have one of the best coaches around and win almost every season." She sighed. "I just have to make the cut."

"So, I'll ask again." He glanced at her. "Are you any good?"

"Yes!" She playfully punched his arm.

"Ouch!" He laughed, then took her hand. "Well, if you're good, then you have nothing to worry about. You'll do great."

He parked against the curb and bent down to look out the passenger window. "The surf looks low."

She laughed. "This coming from a guy who grew up in Florida. Ha! I've seen your baby waves."

"Hey!" He tickled her side, then drew her close. "Don't dis the Keys."

She brushed her lips against his and grinned. "I'm not. I'm insulting your puny ocean." She pulled back and jumped out, laughing.

He opened his door, ran to her side, and grabbed her around the waist. Her legs swung out. He whispered, his warm breath raising the hairs on her neck. "Those are fighting words, Missy. You're asking for it."

She giggled and spun around to face him. "Promise."

He kissed her and chills ran down her arms. He caressed the goose bumps and said, "You are cold."

She shook her head. "Trust me. I'm not." *Not anymore.*

He kissed her on the nose. "Let me grab a blanket from the trunk." He opened the back and pulled out a Mexican blanket, then led her down the path to the sand. Seagulls scoured the sky above, families splashed in the waves, but few surfers coasted on the "puny" waves.

Melena eased onto the warm, soft earth and breathed in the salty air. Dylan sat next to her, his presence felt. "It's a beautiful day," she said.

"Yes it is."

She sensed his stare and could feel the crimson stain seeping into her cheeks. "I was talking about the ocean."

He laughed. "Oh. Yeah, it's pretty too."

She leaned back on her elbows and squinted at him through the shade caused by his shadow. "Tell me something no one would expect about you."

"Hmm? Something no one would expect..." He rolled over on his elbows and positioned himself to face her. "That's tough. I'm an open book."

"No you're not."

"Yes, I am. What you see is what you get."

A beach ball rolled over her foot and she threw it back to a portly kid. "Then you are a mystery. Because that is what I see."

"It's hot today." He sat up, pulled his T-shirt off, and wrapped it like a handkerchief around his head. Melena willed herself not to blush as she perused his defined chest.

"Okay, what do you want to know?"

She crossed her arms. "Okay. Out of all the girls at camp, why'd you decide to hang out with me?"

He licked his lips, then smiled. "I liked the fact you blush."

Heat rose up her back and out to every limb. She looked away.

He touched her chin and angled it to face him. "I knew within minutes of meeting you that you had depth. In a way, you get me, and therefore, I get you. You're beautiful, and I can't stop thinking about you."

Her insides melted. *Boy, you know just what to say, don't you?* She sighed. "Okay, that's good."

"Wouldn't want you to blush again?"

She pinched her lips together and marked in the sand. "So, do you have a job?"

"I did. In Florida, I worked at the Chicken Shack."

She laughed. "Did you wear a uniform?"

"Um, well, they had a chicken mascot costume." He mimed the shape of beak and a big belly with wings.

"Classic. Did you have to wear it?"

He rolled his eyes, but didn't answer.

"I bet you did." She smiled. "Do have pictures?"

"If I did, do you think I'd share them with you?"

She kissed his nose and ran for the water.

He followed behind her.

As water lapped at her feet, she sprang back to dry land. "It's freezing!"

"Nonsense." He plunged straight into a wave and screamed like a girl. "Oh my gosh, that's cold."

She laughed. "That'll teach you not to believe me." Melena kicked at the surf, spraying his chest with water.

"Oh, you're going to get it."

He took after her down the beach. She glanced over her shoulder at the man in pursuit and couldn't remember a day when she'd had more fun.

****

Dylan walked Melena to the front door and took her in his arms. "I think I could really fall hard for you."

She touched her lips to his, assuring him she felt the same.

He hugged her close, and then said, "I'll see you Saturday."

"Bye."

Melena floated into the house, shut the door, and sighed. She turned and the bliss vanished.

Her sister stood poised like a lioness ready to pounce.

"What do you want, Cassi?"

She put her arm around Melena's shoulders and led her into the living room. "Just wondering how my favorite sister is doing?"

Melena recoiled. "Okay, what are you up to?"

"Nothing." Cassi crossed her legs and folded to the floor.

"Yeah, right. Are you forgetting something?"

"What? Dylan?" She blew through her lips. "You can have him if you want."

Melena narrowed her eyes. *There's no way. Cassi never gives up this easy.* "What are you up to, Cassandra?"

"Nothing. Gracious, Mel. Chill." Cassi pulled an old high-school yearbook into her lap. "But I do wonder something. Could you ever fall in love with him?"

"Who?"

"You know who?"

"Dylan?"

Cassi shook her head and pointed to a picture in the yearbook.

Melena stepped over and glanced down at the pages. Cassi's manicured nail rested on a snapshot of

Jason Meals—the school techno-nerd. Melena danced one time with him at a spring dance, mainly because she felt sorry for him. She laughed. "Are you kidding? No. You know that. I only hung out with him because I couldn't bring myself to tell him the truth. Trust me. He's not my type."

"Hmmm? I thought for sure you liked him. I guess that means I can date him if I want to." She snapped the book closed and got up.

"Knock yourself out."

Cassi gathered the yearbook, sheets of music, and her phone, and scurried up the stairs.

Melena opened her laptop and scrolled through Facebook. She considered posting, but decided not to share just yet. For a moment, she looked away from the screen and stared at the spot where her sister had just been. Her senses were heightened at the thought of Cassi being so nice. *What is she up to?* Melena ran a hand over her face and sighed. *Stop it! You asked God to help your relationship with your sister. Maybe this is the first step.* But her gut screamed foul play. Cassi had never been her friend.

****

Cassi spent the rest of her day on a mission. To find Dylan Hart's address. After a few phone calls and a moment on MapQuest, she was ready.

As she pulled up in the taxi, she could hear the loud thump of bass coming from the apartment. *Hmm? Likes his music loud.* She asked the cab driver to stay put and stepped down the walkway, almost unable to contain her giddiness. *This is going to work, and he's going to be mine.* She took a deep breath and glanced at her reflection in the bay window. Her dark hair looked cute pulled back in a ponytail and her size three figure glowed in a white summer dress. *Yeah, you're straight up fine. He won't be able to resist you.* She ran a hand over her hip and punched the doorbell with her thumb.

He opened the door and scowled. "Cassi. What do you need?"

"Hi, Dylan." *Okay, so he doesn't look happy with me yet.* She fingered her phone in her purse. *He will.* "What I need is for you to let me in. I have something I think you should hear."

He hesitated and Cassi pushed past him. She stopped in the middle of the living room and glanced around. Next to the door stood an antique cherry-wood desk that matched the end tables adorning a high-backed green couch. Across from it were a marble fireplace, an indoor tree, and an old grandfather clock.

"Nice pad. So homey."

Dylan crossed his arms and faced her. "What do you want, Cassi?"

"Obviously, small talk is out. I guess I'll just get to the point." She reached in her bag and withdrew her phone. "Well, it just so happens I was taping my voice for my singing coach, when my sister came home from her date with you." She sat on the edge of the couch. "I decided we needed to start over, develop a relationship with one another. That is, until she said…what she said about you." She took a step toward him. "I really like you, Dylan, and I won't let my sister hurt you."

"What are you talking about?"

"Listen." She pressed play.

Dylan leaned against the wall as the message played.

"Could you ever fall in love with him?"

"Who?"

"You know who?"

"Dylan…Are you kidding? No. You know that. I hung out with him because I couldn't bring myself to tell him the truth. Trust me. He's not my type."

"Hmmm? I thought for sure you liked him. I guess that means I can date him if I want to."

"Knock yourself out."

Cassi pressed stop and studied Dylan's face. His cheeks were beat red, his jaw clenched, his eyes jaded. She had succeeded.

"I think you should leave," he said.

What? "But I thought…"

He turned away. "Just go, Cassi."

She stuffed her phone back in her purse and walked to the door. "If you need anything…anything at all. I'm here for you."

He didn't face her.

She shut the door, stunned. Slowly, she moved back to the taxi. *That didn't go as I expected.* Cassi climbed in the car. "349 Delmar Heights," she said to the driver. *But even if he doesn't go for me, I still win. Melena doesn't get him either. Ha!* She pulled her iPod out of her purse, inserted her earphones, and blasted the music, leering all the way back home.

****

Dylan walked the two blocks to the ocean. The sun was still high and beachcombers lined the sand like beached whales. His feet dug into the soft earth as he sulked to the water's edge. He sat on the wet sand, stuck his legs out in front of him, and allowed the tide to lap at his feet. The peaceful landscape seemed surreal to the pyre in his heart.

On his left, an elderly couple waded in the ocean, laughing and kissing as the waves hit their backs. They appeared so happy. So in love. But they were the lucky ones, weren't they? *Maybe love like that doesn't exist anymore.*

Just that morning, he had thought he'd possibly had the start of that, too. He closed his eyes and sighed.

A hand slapped Dylan's back and he jumped.

"Dude, what are you doing?" Chad said, coming around him.

Dylan stared down at his soggy shorts and frowned. "Bad day."

"What happened?"

His muscles tensed. "I found out Melena only dated me because she didn't want to hurt my feelings."

His friend squatted next to him and lifted his sunglasses to the top of his head. "What makes you think that?"

"Cassi came over and played a message. I guess she was recording her voice lessons and forgot to turn it off." Dylan squinted against the sun. "Melena said she wasn't interested and she only went out with me because she didn't have the heart to tell me the truth."

"So you think she was leading you on?"

Dylan shot to his feet. "That's precisely what I think."

"I don't know, man." Chad stood, shaking his head. "That doesn't sound like her."

"How would we even know? We've only known her for what? A few weeks."

"She kissed you, right?"

"Yeah, so?"

"Well, I think that should say something in her

defense." Chad placed a hand over his eyes to shield the sun. "I think you should call her and hear her side."

A piece of seaweed washed up on the shore. Dylan stepped on it and cracked open the rust-colored bulb. He stared in fascination as the seawater drizzled out the wound. *Maybe I should call her. See what she'd say.* He sighed. Maybe Chad was right. Maybe it was a misunderstanding. Maybe...

"No! If I ask her, she'll only deny it. If she didn't have the nerve to tell me the truth before, she sure won't tell me now." He tossed the strand of seaweed back into the water and ran down the beach. *I heard the truth with my own ears. She said it with her own mouth.*

Chapter Ten

Melena carried her cell phone with her for days. She also stayed near her landline, just in case, not venturing farther than the bathroom or kitchen. Every time the phone rang, or the cell phone chirped, she leapt for it. No such luck. Telemarketers, the church, her mom's clients, April, and Nick; it seemed everybody but Dylan knew her number.

Why hasn't he called? Everything seemed perfect this time. She pouted. *Of course, that's it. Too perfect.* He even missed their date on Saturday. Her stomach was too sick to eat, yet too hungry not to eat something. Sleep evaded her and her head pounded from crying. April finally came over to assess the damage.

"Why haven't you called me back? And why didn't you show up for church?" April knocked the door closed. "Look at you. You're a mess."

"I didn't want to leave or tie up the line in case Dylan called."

"You could have instant messaged me." She flopped to the couch and tossed her bag under the coffee table. "You can't let this guy get to you. You've got to get out of this house."

"No, I have to be here if he calls."

"Mel, this isn't the 1950s. Why don't you just call him?"

She shook her head and focused on the sharp, glass

corner of the coffee table. *Because if he liked me, he would have called me like he said. Because I won't give him the satisfaction.* She buried her head in her hands. *Because it hurts too much.*

"Have you looked at yourself lately?" April pointed to the living room mirror.

Melena stared at her face. Her eyes were bloodshot framed by dark circles. Her cheeks were pale and her hair matted.

"You look like you've had the kiss of death," April said to her reflection.

"Well, for days now, I haven't had the kiss of Dylan." Melena dropped to the ground and allowed the tears to fall. Her gut wrenched. *Why hasn't he called?*

"Okay, that's it. I'm going over there now. No guy is going to do this to my best friend and get away with it." She jumped up, snatched her purse, and flung open the door. "I'm going to get to the bottom of this. You stay put and I'll be back in an hour."

"What are you going to do?"

"No worries." She pointed to a bowl of Kisses on the counter. "Eat some chocolate. I'll be back." April pinched her lips together in a compassionate smile and flew out the door.

Melena sat stunned.

About a half hour later, there was movement at the front door. She looked at her watch. *That was fast.* "Come in, April."

Nick and Keith entered.

"Nick. Keith. Um…hi." Melena wiped her eyes, ran fingers through her disheveled hair and pulled at her T-shirt. "What are you two doing here?"

"Melena, where have you been?" Keith faced her

with crossed arms. "Volleyball club tryouts are today. You were supposed to meet Kelly and me first thing this morning."

"You drove over an hour just to tell me that. You couldn't call?"

"You didn't answer your cell and the phone is off the hook," Nick said, eyeing the extension on the counter.

Her heart fell into her stomach. She snatched up the living room line and pressed "talk." No dial tone. Her pulsed raced. Maybe Dylan had called and she'd missed it. The blood rushed to her skull. Frantic, she searched for the misplaced line. *Cassi's room.* Melena bolted upstairs and into the den of the devil incarnate. Sure enough, it was off the hook.

"Nice!" She slammed the receiver and groaned, "What a jerk."

The guys met her in the doorway.

Nick crossed his arms and stepped forward. "Anything you'd like to explain?"

She bit the side of her cheek, mustering the courage to be direct with her brother. "Look, I'm sorry you two drove all the way down here, but I'm not going."

They exchanged glances. She had talked about the club tryouts almost every day, until...well, until camp. Dylan had sort of shadowed her first love—volleyball. Melena wasn't in the mood to play at the present, and now that she knew the phone was off the hook, she didn't want to miss his call.

"You can't be serious?" Keith stepped forward. "You'll miss your shot to play for the season." He glanced at Nick. "Something would have to be terribly wrong for her to give that up without a fight."

Melena nudged them into the hall and shut her sister's door. "It's not a big deal."

"Yes, it is," Keith said. "You've worked too hard to get that spot. If you don't go today, you can kiss volleyball good-bye."

"So, what? Big-D."

"Nick, talk some sense into your sister, please."

Keith's dad had been Melena and Kelly's coach for four years. Because of his dad coaching and these two girls, Keith had invested in them physically and never missed a game. He cared whether or not she went.

"Melena, what's going on?" Nick furrowed his eyebrows. "You're talking nonsense."

She couldn't hold back the painful emotion any longer. The dam broke and tears flowed. "Dylan hasn't called. He didn't show up Saturday for our date, and I don't know why."

Nick glanced from Melena to Keith and back to Melena. "Who's Dylan?"

"He's the guy Mel's been seeing." Keith bit the corner of his lip. "Well, that is until he switched girls."

Melena sniffed. "What?"

Keith cleared his throat. "I think he's been hanging out with your younger sister lately."

Bile rose in her throat. "How do you know?"

"I saw them together at the mall on Sunday." He glanced at Nick. "Rumor is he's taking her to the end-of-the-summer banquet."

Nick's jaw clenched. "That girl."

"But that's impossible." Fresh tears lined her lashes. The room spun. "He asked me!"

"Come on." Nick took Melena's hand and led her

to the bedroom. "Get ready." His mouth tight, his eyes on fire. It was no secret he thought Cassi was a spoiled brat. They'd never gotten along. He loved Melena best, and she knew there was no way he'd stand for this.

But the thought of leaving the phone scared her. *What if they're wrong? What if he really has been trying to call?* But he had her email address, didn't he? He knew where she lived. If he wanted to, he could have reached her. Right? What if it wasn't right?

"I really don't want to leave."

"You're not going to spend one more second feeling sorry for yourself, Mel. You do, and they win. Now get dressed." Nick nodded for Keith to follow him downstairs.

Melena sighed and turned to her room. She dug around in the drawer and found her volleyball uniform from high school. *I hope it still fits.* She pulled on the sleeveless jersey and black polyester shorts. It was snug, but still comfortable. She started for the bathroom, but stopped when she overheard the guys talking.

"I can't believe Cassi belongs to the same family as me. That girl has no feelings whatsoever. When I get my hands on her, I'm going to ring her neck."

She grinned and returned to the task of getting ready. She combed her hair into a ponytail and added a light layer of make-up to her face. She walked back in her room and located the kneepads buried under her bed. *This is supposed to be the most exciting day of my year.* She frowned at her reflection and left to join the lynch party.

"Ready?" Nick said.

"I suppose."

She wrote a note for April to join them at the gym and stuck it on the door. On the way, the boys kept the conversation light, talking about the San Diego sand and grass volleyball clubs versus the ones in Orange County. Though Melena had done her homework on both, she did little talking—no matter how much she was coaxed.

"They actually play four on the court?" Keith said, pulling his truck into the lot.

Melena ducked out of the car and allowed a smile to play on her lips. The event she'd anticipated. Volleyball players mingled in front of the gym door. Big banners welcomed club members and visitors. A large black and red registration sign hung over a table in front. Thankfully, enthusiasm began to creep into her chest. For two years, she'd been signed up to join the most prestigious club team—the Division A, Spikers. The call came in May. Tryouts were early August.

She pulled her duffel bag from the truck, not taking her eyes from the line of people entering the gym door. Last year, Melena had been disappointed. Captain in her varsity high school, she thought she'd land a prime spot, but she ended up in Division B with the Toros. Not that the Toros were bad, they were actually ranked second in the league. But she had a plan. Since she saw a game with Nick years ago, she had wanted to be one of the Division A, Spikers.

"I'm going to go find Kelly," Keith said. "See you inside."

She nodded and moved into the registration line.

Nick came up beside her. "Nervous?"

She half-smiled. "Only because my mind isn't in the game and I haven't worked out in weeks."

He looked past her, then turned, and glanced around the open lot. "I'm thirsty. I'm going to get a soda. Want anything?"

She shook her head and moved forward in the line.

"I'll be back." He walked through the gym door and out of sight.

Melena sighed. *What am I doing?* The fact she'd allowed a guy to dictate her destiny weighed on her. *I want this. I've wanted this for years. How dare I allow Dylan to take that from me?* She rolled her shoulders back, then cracked her neck side to side.

"Hey gorgeous," came a voice ahead her.

She glanced up.

Her friend, Enrique, stood one person in front of her, smiling. He waved for the girl between them to go in front of him, then stepped next to Melena. A small goatee pinched his dark chin and his shoulder-length black hair was pulled into a ponytail. For years, his presence had made her heart accelerate, but now—a dull thump. *Dylan, what are you doing to me?* "Hey, Enrique," she said with forced enthusiasm.

He frowned. "My, aren't we chipper today."

"Sorry. I'm just having a bad month. How was your trip to Europe?"

"Great!" He inched forward in the line. "Are you free for lunch?"

She glanced over her shoulder. Nick and Keith walked her way. "Sure, if it's okay with my brother."

"Great." He smiled. "If you can make it, meet me in the cafeteria in twenty minutes."

She admired him for a moment. His dark eyes crinkled when he smiled, smooth brown skin glowed from a lot of time in the sun. *Okay, you're still fine.*

She glanced down at the form in his hand. "Are you trying out this year? I thought your arm was bad."

Enrique twisted his wrist over and lifted it up. "I was given a green light from my doctor."

"Next," a woman behind the long table said.

He turned and handed her his form. She wrote a number in the corner, then passed him a yellow card in return. "Tryouts are at one-thirty."

"I couldn't find Kelly," Keith said as he and Nick came alongside Melena.

Melena gave the same woman her form.

In return, she handed Melena a yellow card. "Tryouts are at four."

Melena glowered. "Four? I thought they were this morning."

"You're trying out for Division A?"

She nodded.

The woman scanned the sheet in front of her. "Four." She then looked past Melena to the person behind her. "Next."

"Great." Melena stepped out of line and faced her friends. "I'm stuck here until after four." What if Dylan called her in the next few hours while she was here? *Stop it, Melena! No more thoughts of Dylan.*

"Hey, would it be okay with you guys if I went to lunch with Enrique?"

Nick glanced around. "Rick's here?"

"Yeah, over there." She pointed to where he stood about ten feet away studying the card in his hand.

Nick sauntered over to him and they knocked knuckles. They talked for a while before Enrique nodded and walked away.

"Man, I missed that guy this summer," Nick said to

Keith. "You know he turned down the chance to compete in the Pipeline Masters to go on that mission trip last Christmas."

"No way." Keith shot a look to where Enrique stood only a moment ago. "He's that good?"

Nick nodded. "The best."

Keith shook his head. "Wow. I don't think I could do it."

"The guy's relationship with God is tight."

Melena toyed with the string on her sweat jacket. "So, would you guys be okay with me ditching you to have lunch with him?"

Nick and Keith exchanged glances. "Yeah, I think that's a good idea," Nick said. "In fact, I told him about the banquet."

She wrinkled her eyebrows. "What? When? Better yet, why?"

"Just a minute ago. He said he wanted to go to lunch with you and I told him you needed an escort to your church end-of-the-summer banquet. He asked what that was, and I told him."

Her head pounded, anger seeped through her system. Melena clicked her tongue on the roof her mouth, trying to calm her response. "Why would you do that, Nick? I'm going with Dylan."

"No you're not."

"You don't know that. How dare you!"

Nick wrapped his arm around her shoulders in some vain attempt to calm her down. "Look, I'm tired of seeing you hurt. You deserve to have a good time. Rick is a great guy."

"Don't you think I know that?" She unraveled from his hold. "I've liked him for years."

He shrugged. "So what's the problem?"

She glanced at Keith. He held up his hands and backed away.

"Come on, Nick. Would you like it if I tried to set you up with someone?"

He glanced around, biting his cheek. "No."

"Okay, then."

"Kelly!" Keith pointed over their shoulders and smiled. "See you two later."

"You're right, Mel. Sorry."

She threw up her hands and let out an exasperated groan. "Okay. I know you're only trying to help. But don't, okay?"

"Okay." He smiled and pulled her in for a hug. "Forgive me."

"There's enough Harrison rivalry going on. I don't need to be mad at you, too." She squeezed him and stepped back.

"Um, now that you forgive me, I have some bad news."

She titled her head, ready for a damaging blow. "What?"

"Don't freak out," Nick put up his hand holding the soda. "But I saw Cassi."

Melena's heart skipped. "What?"

"Yeah, inside." He nodded at the gym.

"What's she doing here? She's not old enough for this club."

"Yeah, that's what I said. But apparently, the club has started a junior league."

Melena grimaced. *Whoo hoo.* "She's staying at Mom's house. Is she planning to commute up here every day?"

Nick stuck out his chest and cocked his head to the side. "I'm not driving her."

Melena mimicked his pose and slapped her hand to her hip. "Well, don't look at me. I'm not driving her either."

They laughed.

"So, how did the diva get up here anyway?"

He shrugged. "Probably talked some poor guy into bringing her."

Melena flinched. She prayed Dylan wasn't Cassi's chauffeur. One glimpse of him and she could kiss Division A good-bye.

Chapter Eleven

Since tryouts weren't for several hours, Melena went to the campus cafeteria excited to see her old friend. She selected a pre-packaged egg salad sandwich and a bottle of water from the cooler, paid, and slid into the booth across from him. "So, Rick, tell me about your summer."

Enrique set his fork down and swallowed. "I first trained with the Campus Disciples in Texas and then went from there to Europe. We traveled to France, Italy, Germany, all over Europe, staying in hostels and on military bases, while working with the local missionaries."

"Is the rumor true? Did you meet someone?"

He smiled. "Tanya is an Army brat. Her father is stationed in Germany. She volunteers with Campus Disciples."

"And…" Melena leaned forward on her elbows.

"And, we got along." He smiled and bit off the end of a fry. "So, tell me about your summer."

"I met someone, too." Her stomach flipped and she shifted her eyes to the table. "Things didn't work out."

"Didn't work out?"

"He's going out with my sister now." Her unsettled voice betrayed her.

"Really?" He crossed his arms and leaned back. "And you still like him? Doesn't say much for his character."

"It doesn't matter." She ran her eyes across the empty cafeteria. "Are you still seeing Tanya?"

He shrugged. "She lives in Europe, and I don't really believe in long distance romances. We agreed to call it what it was. A summer romance."

"Hmm?"

"I missed being here with all my friends so it's good to be back." He held up his hamburger and smiled. "And to have good ole' American food. This is my fourth hamburger this week."

She eyed his plate and grinned. Potato salad, coleslaw, French fries, and baked beans complimented his American meal. "Missed it all, huh?"

"Hey, I was raised on a ranch as a kid. This is my staple."

She laughed and took a sip of her water. "I always thought of you more as a carne asada burrito man."

"That's because burritos were all you ever saw me eat in high school." He scooped beans onto his spoon. "I loved that restaurant on the corner. What was it called?"

She tapped the table, trying to remember. "Rositos, maybe?"

He shrugged. "Well, they had the best food."

Melena grimaced. "I ate there once and puked in English class. Never went back."

He dropped his spoon and slapped his hands together. "That's right. Smelt awful for weeks."

"Thanks," she said with pursed lips.

"Anyways…" He pulled a pickle from his burger, and dropped it on the side of his plate, then cleared his throat. "So, your brother told me about your church end-of-the-summer banquet? Are you going?"

She dropped the crust of her sandwich and exhaled. "Um…no, I don't think so."

"How come?"

Melena shrugged. "I may not have a date."

"Then how about letting me take you?"

Her pulse quickened. *What do I say?* Answering "yes," meant admitting Dylan and she were over. "I'm not sure."

"You're not sure because you aren't going? Or there's someone else? Or I'm a loser?"

She laughed. *Define irony.* She had liked Enrique for years, but he was always oblivious. They'd gone to fairs and movies, ate lunch together almost every day, and he'd never given her a second glance. And, of course, she was too shy to tell him how she felt.

Now that Dylan was in the picture, Enrique seemed interested. *Figures.* "I told Dylan I'd go with him, but that was before…" She poked at the remaining crust on her plate.

"Before he hooked up with Cassi."

She cringed. "Yeah."

"Well, think about it." He touched her hand. "I don't have plans that day and I'd love to go with you."

Her cheeks burned. Of course, Enrique had seen her blush a million times before. Knowing him, he probably said things just to watch the show. She still found him attractive. *Maybe there's something still here.* "Okay. I'll call you."

He checked his watch. "Well, we better get back. I need to stretch before I tryout."

She glanced down at the empty trash on his tray. "Are you going to be able to move?"

He swatted at the air and grinned. "I'll burn this in ten minutes."

She scooted her chair back and pitched her trash in the can by the door.

Enrique escorted her out the door and back to the gym. "Talk at you later."

She waved and watched him walk to one of the courts. The room was filled with the sound of bouncing balls, game chatter, and the squeak of rubber soles on the wood floor. The thick air smelt of sweat socks and lemon oil. It felt great to be back.

She sized up the competition in the room. Most of the women were tall, their calves and biceps taunt. *Can I keep up?* She didn't feel athletic at the moment. *I guess I could always picture Cassi's head as the ball.* That at least made Melena smile.

She pivoted around on her heel and exited through the side door. *Aw, speak of the Devil.* Across the quad, Cassi leaned against a soda machine in animated conversation with some guys. *Why does she always have to be where I am? Can't she get her own life? You're in high school, Cassi.* Melena studied her outfit as she approached. Her sister had on short shorts, a workout bra and an exposed belly ring. *Wouldn't want to keep them guessing.* Melena took a deep breath. *Lord, give me wisdom. Keep me in check.*

"Cassi, what are you doing here?"

She flipped around and flashed a forced smile. "Same as you. Duh."

Melena shook her head. "How do you plan to get up here if you make it on a team?"

She pawed a bald guy to her left. He had to be at least twenty-three. "Blane said he'd give me a ride up."

"Why don't you just join a league in San Diego? Do us all a favor."

She pressed her lips together and smirked. "Afraid of the competition?"

Human weakness wanted to slap her stupid, but a good conscience reminded Melena to love thy enemy. *Big breath in. Remember, she's my sister. Sister, enemy. What's the difference?*

"I have a message for you," Melena said.

Cassi studied her fingernails and yawned. "Yeah, what?"

"Your ex, Carmen, called last night." It was true. He had called. Melena just left out a little detail. He had just called to get a phone number.

Her eyes went wide. "What did he want?"

"To talk to you. I told him you were on a date, though, so you wouldn't be able to talk."

Cassi's stare narrowed. "Anything to hurt me, huh? Well, guess what? I have Dylan now, and that's all that matters."

"Who's paying him to babysit you?"

She crossed her arms, ran her eyes over Melena's body, then sneered. "Yeah, okay." She shifted forward and angled on one hip. "I may be young, but it shows who has it and who doesn't."

Melena glanced around. Their audience had grown. *Better say something clever, or I'll be the laughing stock in the league for the rest of the year.* "No, actually I conceal what I have and you flaunt what you don't. You're a fourteen-year-old kid playing dress up." She switched her gaze to Blane. "You heard me. She's fourteen!" Then she looked back to her sister's soured face. "You're a child in way over your head. Get your own life!" Melena flipped around and pushed through the crowd.

Cassi yelled a few choice words at her back, but Melena didn't care. She had actually stood up to her sister in front of a large group of people without blushing or crying. She peeked at her watch. Less than ten minutes until tryouts. She smiled. With the adrenaline that pulsed through her veins, she should do great.

Chapter Twelve

"Okay, ladies," the coach said to those left in the room. "Everyone take a seat, and I'll hand out the club schedule for this year."

A hush fell as everyone found a place on the bleachers. Melena sat next to Kelly two rows up and wiped at the beads of perspiration on her forehead. She had decided to take a light jog around the campus to cool off from her meeting with Cassi and to warm up for her tryout. A stack of schedules came down the row. Melena took one and passed it on.

"This is such a formality," Kelly whispered. "Everyone is going to make the team. Don't worry."

"Where'd you hear that?" Melena whispered. "We both tried out last year and ended up on the B team."

She shrugged. "My brother-in-law is on the committee. He said they barely have enough girls signed up this season. So, we'll see."

Melena did a quick inventory. There were at least twenty prospects left in the room. If she wanted to be a Spiker, then she'd have to be in the top twelve.

The room buzzed with chatter. The coach held up her hand. "Now listen up, ladies. I have some disappointing news to share. We only have eight slots left in the club."

Melena's gut wrenched. She shot Kelly a look.

Kelly shrugged.

"Two on the Toros, four on the Jets, one on the Hawks…" She glanced down at her list.

Heat ran down Melena's back. *Please say Spikers.*

"And one on the Spikers."

Yes! Wait. "That's only one slot."

Kelly nudged her elbow. "So, we won't be on the same team. You've got to make it."

"If you don't make the cut, there are Division B coaches in the bleachers. They'd love to talk to you." The coach cleared her throat and withdrew a whistle from her shirt. "Drills everyone. Better keep up if you want to play in the A Division." She blew and the women jumped up.

Melena hurried to the end of the court and pulled her arm over her head for one last stretch. She didn't want to think about another year in the lower league. She eyed last year's coach on the sideline. He nodded. She waved and focused forward. As cool as he was, she wanted Division A. The whistle blew.

Lord, help me.

****

They jogged in place for about ten minutes, ran wind sprints, pumped out about fifty pushups, shuffled, bumped, spiked, set, and blocked. After an hour of intense exercise, the coach sounded the whistle. Most girls dropped to the floor, exhausted.

Melena slumped to the bleachers, drenched in sweat and short of breath. Kelly staggered up next to her and dropped to the bench, panting. "I should have eaten less ice cream this summer and ran more. I need to diet."

"Kelly, please. You're a twig."

Kelly laughed. "And you're not."

"Shh…she's reading the names."

"Lisa Korte and Ruth Van—Toros."

The two girls squealed, the rest held their breath.

"Katherine Moody, Terri Whaling, Julia Fitz, Barbara Meek—Jets."

Melena's head throbbed. Stars sprinkled in front of her eyes. She realized she'd stopped breathing and exhaled.

"Kelly Fitzpatrick—Hawks."

Kelly squealed. "Yes!" She practically fell in Melena's lap.

Melena pushed her off, trying to concentrate on the last name on the list. Kelly squeezed her hand. "Melena Harrison—Spikers."

"Oh my goodness!" Her stomach leapt into her throat. Tears of shock and joy flowed down her cheeks. "I made it!"

"Your uniforms will be available at the first club meeting. Details will be in the mail." The coach tucked the clipboard under her arm. "To everyone else. Thanks for a good work out. Stay and talk with the coaches on the bench, or come see us next year."

"Spikers! Can you believe it?" Melena pinched her arm and lifted the strap of her bag on her shoulder. Her head whirled. "So much has been going wrong. It feels good to have something go right. Yes!"

Kelly squeezed her around the shoulders and led her to the door. "I knew you'd get it. You've been the best for as long as I've known you."

"I can't believe it." Melena pushed the gym doors open. The low, afternoon sun blinded her. She reached in her backpack pocket and withdrew sunglasses. "Know what's weird?"

"What?"

"That God even cares about our dreams."

An African-American girl Melena recognized from the bleachers stepped up behind them. "It's a big deal to get on the Spikers. Do you know what you've gotten yourself into?"

Melena faced her. "I know they have the best coach in the club and they've won almost every year."

The girl nodded. "There is a reason for that."

Melena swallowed. "Have you played under Coach Wilson before?"

"You could say that." The girl retrieved her bag from the ground and swung the strap over her shoulder. "I'm her daughter." And with that, she sauntered away.

Melena stared with her mouth gaped open.

Kelly stuffed her sweatshirt in her gym bag and zipped it closed. "I'm going to go find Keith. I'll catch up with you in a bit, okay?"

"Okay." Melena lay back against a tree and stared up at the sky. Southern California hadn't had rain in a while, so she was surprised the usual brown haze didn't block her view. Other than a small commercial plane that flew overhead, the sky appeared virtually empty. The air was warm and humid. She reached in her bag and withdrew her cell phone. She dialed Nick.

"Hey!"

Melena looked up from her phone and squinted at April standing a few feet away. "When did you get here?"

"About thirty minutes ago. Long enough to hear you're the Spikers' newest star." She squealed and gave Melena a hug.

"Isn't that insane!"

"I knew you could do it." April glanced around the quad, then back at Melena.

"So what did you find out?" Melena asked, afraid of the answer.

April shrugged. "Nothing. Chad's brother said they were at the beach. He didn't know which. I drove around for a while trying to find them. No luck." She pushed a strand of hair over her ear, revealing several earrings. "So, what's up with you and Enrique?"

"You can give me a ride back to Del Mar, right?"

"That's why I'm here. Well, that and to support you, of course."

Melena turned on her phone. "Then give me a second to call Nick."

"Don't avoid the question." Her friend crossed her legs and popped open a can of soda. "Nick tells me you ate lunch with him. Something is up."

Melena grinned. "Nick had him ask me to the banquet."

"What?" April lifted an eyebrow. "Does he like you?"

"I guess."

"Wow." April took a swing from her can.

"Okay, why does that surprise you? You said yourself, I'm hot."

"Oh, I know you're hot." She laughed. "But you've harbored this tanker crush on him since the ninth grade, and he never even noticed."

Melena rolled her eyes. "Well, I think he notices me now."

"That's so typical."

"I know." Melena fell backward on the lawn and threw hands in the air.

April laughed.

Melena fingered a tall piece of grass and met her friend's gaze. "Should I go?"

"Hmm? Do you still like him?"

Do I? "No idea. I'm too numb right now to say."

April toyed with the ring on her can and smirked. "Who knew my best friend was such a boy magnet?" She began singing a Heavy-D tune bit too loud.

"Okay, you can stop that right now."

April nudged Melena's calf with her foot.

Melena countered by tossing a pebble at her. It plinked on top of the can and landed in the hole. Melena hid a laugh behind her hand. "Whoops."

"Oh great, Mel. Thanks a lot." April kicked her leg playfully again.

"It's added flavor."

"Yeah, whatever, Melena."

The two women pretended not to be amused, then both broke into hysterics. It felt good to laugh and get off the roller coaster of emotion.

"So, is your mom going to let you stay the rest of the summer with me or what?"

April exhaled through her nose. "I don't know. She's on a really funny kick right now. I think she is having a hard time letting me go." April poured the remainder of her soda on the roots of the tree. "I guess I understand, but it's inevitable. She can't stop it." She stood and smashed her can with her foot. "You ready to head back down?"

Melena spotted Enrique at the edge of the parking lot. "Yeah, in a second. Where are you parked?"

April pointed over her shoulder and backed up. "Out in Timbuktu. Couldn't find a spot."

"Okay, I'll meet you there in a second."

"Okay." April gathered her trash and started for the car.

Enrique caught Melena's line of sight and walked toward her. "How'd it go?"

She rolled her shoulders up, then screamed. "I made it! Division A, Spikers."

He smiled. "Never doubted you for a second."

"And you?"

"Division B, Co-ed mix."

She lowered her lip in a pout. "I'm sorry. But it's still fun, right?"

He flared his nostrils, then grinned. "Yeah. It's cool."

"Probably all that food."

He laughed.

A warm breeze blew across the nape of her neck and she closed her eyes. "Ah...that feels good. That gym was like a hundred degrees."

"Over three hundred bodies were sweating in there. I was more concerned about the smell."

Melena smiled. She stared at him. His dark eyes and firm features still attracted her, but she didn't know if she felt the same about him. Dylan was clouding her emotions. She couldn't let the shade of confusion speak for her. "How about we get together Sunday afternoon and figure out our plans for the banquet?"

A huge grin swept across his face. "So, you'll go with me then?"

She shrugged. "Sure. It'll be fun."

"I'll pick you up around two, okay?"

She nodded. "Well, I'd better go. April is waiting for me at the car. See you Sunday."

He put out his arms for a hug.

She pulled out her sweat drenched T-shirt and scrunched her nose. "I'm kind of a mess."

He shrugged. "Me, too."

She gave him a quick hug and stepped back. She wished Enrique had shown interest before Dylan. Maybe then this wouldn't be so hard.

"Bye, Melena."

She waved and walked down the hill to the blacktop. A new weight pressed on her chest. If Dylan called now, what would she say? She stopped on the sidewalk feet apart, fists clenched, squeezing her eyelids shut. *Augh! Boys stink! Big breath in. Not going to start the "what-ifs." Pulling myself together.* She inhaled and held the air. Then pushed it out in a rush.

"You okay?" April yelled over the roof of her car.

Melena opened her eyes and shot her fist in the air. "Yes, I just made it on the Spikers. Whoo hoo!"

"Come on. Let's get out of here." April laughed as she climbed in the car and started the engine.

Melena stepped off the curb and joined her. "I thought dating was supposed to be fun."

April chuckled and pulled out of the driveway. "If it was, there would be no country music."

Melena sniggered. "Funny." She lit up the screen of her cell phone and called Nick. He didn't pick up, so she left a message. "Hey, I'm going home with April. That way you don't have to drive me back. Oh and I'm a Spiker." She squealed, "Bye." She pushed end call and stared out the side window.

Melena's excitement was shadowed by the questions that plagued her mind. She wanted answers. *Why did Dylan stand me up? Why is he dating Cassi?*

Why can't I forget about Dylan and fall head over heels for Enrique again? She sighed. *Because my heart doesn't have enough room.*

Chapter Thirteen

Melena came home from church and plopped down on the bed. Dylan hadn't showed for service. Maybe he had changed churches, all on account of her. She didn't feel like doing anything but lying here feeling sorry for herself all day. But that wouldn't do. She needed to pack. Her dad would be bringing Kevin back any day and she needed to clear out.

She flipped her legs over the edge and slumped to the ground so her chin rested on the mattress. *I'm hopeless*. Her eye caught the Van Gogh painting above her bed. She stood and pulled the pin from the wall. The picture sailed down to the pillow. She stared at the swirling blue lines and thought about Van Gogh's emotions when he painted it. *Did he feel helpless like me?*

Enough wallowing. She grabbed her suitcases out of the closet and tossed them open on the bed. Then retrieved some boxes from the hall closet. Maybe it was a good thing this day had come. She could get on to her normal life, far from Cassi and her memory of Dylan. Without much organization, Melena began tossing clothes, books, and CDs in the various containers. Her gaze lingered on the hoodie on the floor. Melena's heart lurched. She reached for the hoodie and brought it to her nose. Dylan's smell still lingered in the folds.

The phone rang.

She tossed the hoodie on the bed and went to answer it.

Cassi was shopping with their mom, so Melena took it in her sister's room. "Hello?" Nothing. "Hello?"

"Is Cassi there?" *Dylan?*

Her stomach flipped. She opened her mouth to speak, but her voice caught in her throat. "Uh…no. Can I… Do you…" *Get control, Melena.* "Can I take a message?" Her heart pounded like a happy dog's tail. She wanted to scream, "Why don't you love me anymore?" But instead, said nothing.

Silenced ruled for an uncomfortable second or two, before he said, "No, thanks," and hung up.

She sank to the floor with the phone receiver held to her chest. Tears flowed down her cheeks and snot seeped from her nose. Sniffing, she glanced around for a tissue. Only clothes and shoes lined the carpet. A brown T-shirt lay to her left. Her eyes narrowed and she seized it. With a giggle in her throat, she blew her nose on the cotton material. An eerie sense of satisfaction washed over her. She crumpled the shirt and stuffed it at the bottom of a clothes pile. *It'll be nice and crusty by the time she uses it.*

She stood and walked back to her room. But instantly a thrust of guilt flooded her. *I can't do it. I'm not her.* Melena traipsed back into Cassi's room, dug under the heap, and retrieved her "snot rag." *This is why nice girls always finish last.* Melena went back to her room and tossed the shirt in her hamper. She put her arms in Dylan's hoodie, pulled her journal from under the mattress, and sank to the floor with her back to the bed. She flipped to an empty page and wrote.

Jesus, I know I haven't handled this well. I need to

be shown how to love my sister. But look at my Goliath. It will take more than a stone to bring her down. Forgive my attitude.

She lifted her pencil and giggled. *And the snot incident.*

****

Numb, Dylan turned off his cell phone and stuffed it in his jean pocket. He was returning a call to Cassi. When he heard Melena's voice, his heart stopped. First reaction, he was glad. Then memories and anger clambered in. Why didn't she say something? Admit something that would indicate he was wrong about her. But Melena didn't say anything. Acted cold, even.

Dylan stretched out on his bed and stared at the ceiling. His heart ached. *God, you worked so much out in me at the camp. Don't let me fail you now.* He fought against the urge to be angry. But often the rage advanced its score. The game—zero and ten.

What's the big deal? I only went out with her a couple of times. He flipped over and stared at the wall, willing the memories to dissipate. But her flowing blonde hair and gorgeous green eyes stared back at him with every waking second. Why am I stuck on her? He rubbed a hand over his face and exhaled. *Because the few days with her were more natural than my whole relationship with Renee.*

Melena was sweet, fun to tease, easy to talk to— and beautiful—yeah, that too. But it was all fake, wasn't it? *She didn't want to hurt my feelings.* He cringed. How did she think it would end? After all, he kissed her. More than once.

Dylan stayed home from church that morning, afraid he'd run into her. He knew that couldn't last. He shouldn't allow a girl to mess with his relationship with God. Of course, that was probably why he was in such a funk today. He felt betrayed. Chad said Melena had never had a boyfriend because she was shy, but now Dylan knew different. She wasn't shy. She was manipulative.

His phone buzzed in his pocket. It was Cassi. He rolled his eyes. He didn't really want to talk to her. He knew why she was calling. She wanted to go to the banquet together. Why, he wasn't sure. She didn't even attend their church. Well, since she was a kid, so he'd been told.

"Hi, Cassi."

"Hey, Dylan. I know you said you didn't want to go to the banquet..."

Cassi yammered on. He wasn't exactly sure what she was saying. He knew he didn't like her. He liked her sister. Maybe that's why he didn't totally blow her off. A part of him latched onto her for a connection to Melena. He asked about her all the time, but Cassi hardly answered.

"...So you see, even though Melena will be there, I promise she won't bug you."

His heart recessed for a second. Melena would be there. "She's still going?"

"Yeah, but like I said. She won't bother us."

Dylan considered this. He had turned Cassi down before, but now, maybe he'd go. *For revenge? Or because I want to see Melena one last time?* He sighed. Revenge sounded good. But as sure as his chest rose and fell, he knew it was the latter.

****

The doorbell rang.

Oh no. Melena glanced at her watch. *Oh no!* "Just a minute," she yelled down the stairs. She ran to the bathroom mirror and gasped horrified. *I look like a raccoon.* She grabbed a towel from the rack and wiped under her eyes. *Better, but there is nothing I can do about my red nose.* She sighed. *It will have to do.* She skipped down the stairs and flung open the door.

Enrique studied her face. "Melena, what's wrong?"

"Oh, it's just Cassi again. Nothing I can't handle." She swiped at the air. "Ready?"

He opened his arms and Melena stepped into them for a hug. He was so warm. *Maybe I have the better deal.* "So, what do you want to do?"

"I was thinking we could go to the mall and pick out outfits."

He pulled back with a raised eyebrow. "You aren't serious?"

"What? It'll be fun." She glanced at her watch. "Ooh, and we better get before the stores close." Melena grabbed her purse from the kitchen counter.

"You're going to owe me one. I wouldn't go shopping with just any girl."

She grinned. "Come on."

He nodded and walked her to his Accord. Once they were settled, he asked, "When are you moving back to your dad's house? The hour drive is a killer."

"Wednesday, I think. It depends on whether or not Kevin is ready to switch." She buckled her seat belt and looked at him. "Cassi has decided to stay in Del Mar this year with my mom. Nick is staying in Fullerton."

"I heard a rumor April was going to room with you this year."

"She wanted to, but her mom wasn't thrilled with

the idea. I think she will at least stay for a few weeks until high school starts."

He pulled onto the freeway and an adjusted the air conditioner. "It's cool you two have remained such great friends all these years."

Melena smiled. "Yeah, she's the sister I never had."

"Yeah." Enrique nodded with a grin. "Nick must be real stoked about staying with you."

"Yeah, well, he didn't really like being away from his friends, and to be truthful, he doesn't really like living with my mother. Not that any of us do." She glanced out at the afternoon traffic. "He's going to school with me this year and transferring to UCLA next fall."

He slowed almost to a standstill, then glanced at her. "What does he want to be?"

"Well, he's always been a drama king, so I'm guessing theatre."

"Drama king? Really? I always thought he was shy."

"Nick?" She laughed. "Maybe to strangers, one-on-one. Get him in front of a large audience and he's in the zone."

The traffic picked up and they moved over into the carpool lane. "So, is your dad still a minister?"

"Yeah, sort of. Things got kind of messed up for him in the divorce."

"I know your dad stepped down, but he still goes there right?"

"He did until he moved up there."

"Is your mom still involved in the church?"

"Are you kidding?" Melena snorted, then covered

her mouth. "Sorry. I shouldn't say it like that."

He laughed.

"Actually, she claims to be an atheist, but I doubt that. Atheists don't pray when they need money."

"She needs money? I thought she was rich."

"Yeah, well, it takes a lot of cash to support her and Cassi's fashion addiction."

"Have you ever tried talking to your mom and Cassi?"

"We try, but they really don't care. Especially, my sister. She's caught up in some New Age stuff. She checks to see if the moon and stars are aligned before getting her hair cut." She laughed. "Okay, maybe I'm exaggerating."

They drove the rest of the hour in comfortable silence. He turned up the volume of a new Seventh Day Slumber CD and rolled down the window. She turned and watched the picturesque graffiti wiz by. Melena wasn't like most of her friends. As long as there wasn't much traffic, she didn't mind the ride from Del Mar to Fullerton. If she was with a friend, it meant time to talk. If she was alone, it meant time to pray.

The mall appeared on their right, and he signaled to get over. At the exit, the light was green and he turned left into parking structure. "There are a lot of people here today." He flowed in and out of lanes, trying to find an empty space.

Red taillights flashed in a spot to their right. "There's one."

He signaled, waited, and then pulled in.

He came around to open her door and offered his hand.

"Thank you."

Inside, the mall was hopping with activity. Cliques lined the walkways, mothers pushed their strollers with determination, and couples sauntered to their own beat.

Enrique whispered in her ear. "You better hope no one sees me here shopping like one of your girlfriends."

She smiled. "You know you just want to spend time with me."

"Do you think I'd be here otherwise?"

She shook her head and pointed to a small boutique with gold and silver dresses displayed in the window. "Let's go in there." Melena studied the rack, filled with taffetas and silks, in an array of colors. She'd never been a big shopper. That was her sister and Mom's department. Most of Melena's clothes came from her mother's insatiable desire for her to be like Cassi. What Melena bought for herself could be found at any discount department store. A place her sister wouldn't be caught dead in. "What color should I get?"

Enrique leaned against the wall, with his arms crossed. "I think you're on your own. Fashion isn't my thing."

"Hmmm...okay, fine." She slid the hangers across the pole and fingered the assorted fabrics and stopped at a tea-length cream chiffon dress with spaghetti straps. "I think I've found it." She ran her hand over the delicate champagne-colored ribbon that lined the dress. "I'm going to try this one." She went to an open room and pulled it on. It hugged her figure like it was made to measure. Running her hand over her hips, she swiveled around from one side to the other. She stepped out and caught Enrique's eye.

He let out a low whistle. "You're right. That's the one."

The sales-lady approached, nodded, and handed her a matching ivory scarf. "Here, try this."

Melena placed it around her neck, letting the ends drape down her back. *I've got to have this dress.* The price hung from the armpit. She lifted her arm, and then the string. It was on sale for $64. She turned to the saleslady and asked, "Can I put it on layaway?"

"I can only hold it for a week."

Melena went back in the changing room, stepped out of the dress, and back into her jeans, not once taking her eyes from the dress. The light-rose baroque design gave the cream dress a slight vintage appearance. She slipped it on its hanger and touched the material one more time. Smooth like cream.

She carried it out front and laid it on the counter. "I'll be back before Friday."

The lady wrapped it in a plastic bag and took her name.

"Well, Rick," Melena said as she looped her arm with his, "Let's see what the men's shop has in store for you."

He reached down and took her hand in his. She forced a smile, then focused on the spotted tile. The butterflies in the stomach, the swooning of the head, the sweaty palms, the flip of the heart, all of those feelings Dylan initiated in her—none of them were there. *I might as well be holding Nick's hand.*

Enrique pointed to Brian's Tux Shop. "How about here?"

"Are you sure you want to get a tux? You could just wear a suit." Melena asked. "It's just a church banquet."

"Sure, why not."

Thankful for the distraction, Melena let go of his hand and pretended to be interested in a display of cummerbunds.

Enrique studied a mannequin dressed in white with a blue ruffled shirt. "What should I get?"

She shook her head and laughed. "Definitely not that one." She led him to a double-breasted black tux in the corner. "Something like that with a cream colored shirt and tie."

He nodded and gave his order to the man behind the counter. The man escorted him to the back room to take his measurements. By the time they finished and left the shop, the rest of the stores were already rolling down their gates. The parking lot was fairly deserted. "It's been fun," he said, once they'd reached his car.

Melena climbed in, fastened her seatbelt, and pulled her purse into her lap.

Enrique got in and they were off. The conversation was light on the way back. When they hit San Diego County, Enrique pointed to a sign just off the freeway. "Would you mind if we stop at In and Out and grab some burgers? I'm starving, and I haven't had one of those in years."

She shook her head. "Not at all."

They exited to the drive-thru and sat in line. "Do you want anything?"

"Maybe just a shake. I'm not that hungry."

He nodded and ordered their food. After they paid and got their order, he pulled over to the curb. "Here's your shake."

She took the cold drink and took a sip. The thick consistency slowly made its way up the straw. "Mmm. That's good."

Enrique set his box of food on the floorboard and turned to her. "Do you remember when we first met?"

"How could I forget?" She smiled. "You were hall monitor and caught me ditching study hall."

"I have a confession."

She raised an eyebrow. "What's that?"

"I wasn't on hall duty. I saw you and asked Michael if I could borrow his hall monitor arm band."

"What? You're joking?"

He shook his head. "I've liked you since the ninth grade."

You've got to be kidding! Her stomach flipped. "That's crazy." She toyed with a strand of her hair.

"Why is it so crazy? You were the most attractive girl at Claremont High."

Her cheeks began their usual light show and she looked away. *Why now? This doesn't feel right.* "I don't know what to say."

"Sometimes I thought you felt the same. You're a little shy, so I wasn't sure."

She met his eyes. They seemed to search hers. Hopeful for an answer she couldn't give anymore. "I did."

He leaned and touched his lips to hers.

She pulled back. "Wait. I can't."

"But I thought..." Pain and confusion filled his eyes.

How do I tell him the truth without hurting his feelings? How do I tell him the truth, when I don't even know what that is anymore? "Rick, you're right. I liked you for years. But things..." She gazed down at her hand and fiddled with her ring. "I'm still trying to figure things out."

"With Dylan."

She looked back at him and offered a slight grin. "Yeah."

"You deserve better."

She stared out the window, resting her chin on her fist. "You don't even know him."

Enrique turned the key and the engine roared. "He's with your sister, Melena. That's enough."

His words burned her heart. She took a sip of her shake and leaned her head against the window. "I'm not ready to let go."

"Fine." He pulled out into traffic and drove her home without another word.

****

Dylan stood in the In and Out parking lot in shock. He'd spent the afternoon watching a movie with some of Chad's friends. On his way back home, he'd stopped to get a burger. When he stepped from his car, his eyes grazed over the sight of Melena in a car kissing another guy. He stared in disbelief.

He hit the remote for his Jeep and slid behind the wheel. His appetite gone. He had promised the guys to meet up with them later to surf, but he wasn't up to it.

He pulled into the sea of traffic agitated. As he maneuvered around cars, he found himself mumbling "stupid jerk" one too many times. Anger boiled in his skull. He didn't stop at his exit, instead he headed south. The billboards soon turned to Spanish. He didn't care. Maybe a trip to Tijuana was just what he needed.

Why was this girl getting to him so much? He'd known her, how long? Which just angered him even more.

A sign just ahead read, "Imperial Beach." He

swerved his car off the exit and drove until the pavement hit sand. He parked and jumped out of his car, expelling all his frustration in one long sigh.

The afternoon sun made an eerie glow over the tainted waters. Globs of seaweed blanketed the sand. Seagulls lay in masses around the shore. With the exception of a homeless man sleeping next to the fence that bordered Mexico from the U.S., not a soul was in sight.

Dylan fell to ground and closed his eyes. *So, Chad is wrong. Melena played me.* Any hope of misunderstanding was lost with that two-second kiss. And with it, the girl of his dreams.

****

Cassi picked up the phone, but stopped when she heard voices. She covered the mouthpiece.

"Brian, all your stuff is gone. I don't understand," came her mom's voice on the other end. "I thought you loved me."

"Love has nothing to do with this, Rita. You don't even know what that word means."

Her mom sniffed. "I know I love you."

"Love me? How would you define that?"

Cassi slowly shifted her legs under her, trying not to make a noise.

"You're never home and, when you are, you're a cold fish. Loving you is like loving a corpse."

"How can you say that?" she cried. "You can't run out on me. What will I do for money?"

"Ha! Figures that's what would worry you. Good-bye, Rita." He slammed down the phone and the sound of her mother's crying sounded faintly in the receiver.

Cassi slowly set the phone back in its cradle and

stood up. Her feet melted to the floor. *What should I do? Do I go talk to Mom?* She took a step forward, then stopped. Fear clutched her chest. She wouldn't know what to say. Sure, they could talk about Dolce & Gabbana, Christian Dior, and Donna Karan. But about life? Never. The sound of her mother crying rang in her ears. A sound she'd never heard. She inched forward, but an emotional force field kept her at bay. Finally, she turned from the door. *Why do I care? She brought it on herself.*

There was a slight knock at the door.

"Come in," Cassi said.

The door opened and her mother stepped in. "You got a minute?"

****

After offering a lame good-bye to Enrique, Melena closed the front door and sighed. *Why can't I just like him?* It would be so much simpler. *I'm so tired of feeling bad.* She turned to walk up the stairs, when someone knocked. *Good, maybe we can clear the air.* She opened it again. "Kevin!"

He smiled under the weight of boxes. "Hey, sis."

"Moving in?" Melena said, stepping out of his way.

"Yeah. Dad is here with the truck, so you'd better get your things, too." He set his stuff down on the floor and walked back outside.

Cassi came through the kitchen door with a smirk plastered on her face. "Whoops, forgot to tell you Dad called. Guess you're leaving. "

Melena pursed her lips. "Thanks for the warning. I was just up there."

"Any time," she sang, then flipped around, and

disappeared in the kitchen.

At least I'm getting out of here. Melena ran upstairs to grab her things. Luckily, she had already packed the majority of her belongings the night before. She threw the remainder of her stuff in a duffel bag and carried them out to the truck.

Her dad jumped out, tossed them in the truck bed, then gave her a bear hug. "Hi, sweetheart. Need any more help?"

"I only have one more load. I can get it." Melena went in and stopped.

Her mom waited in a nightgown just inside the door. "So, our time is up?"

Melena nodded. "Yeah, I guess so."

"Well, you be a good girl." She touched Melena's shoulder and looked her in the eye. "Be sure to come and visit more this year, okay? I miss you when you're gone."

Melena swallowed as she wrapped the smaller woman in her arms. "Me too, Mom." Surprisingly, her mom didn't feel like a China doll.

For once, she actually hugged her back. "I know I'm not the best mother in the world..." she lifted Melena's chin to face hers, "but I do love you."

"I love you too, Mom." She choked back the tears.

Her mom kissed her cheek, then turned for her room.

Melena blinked, mouth open, eyes watering. *What just happened?*

Cassi stared at her from the stairs. "Don't for a moment think Mom has grown a heart. She's been acting weird all day. Rumor is Brian's leaving her."

"What?" Melena sniffed. "Why?"

Her sister shrugged. "Beats me. Personally, I'm grateful." She skipped the rest of the way up the steps and closed the bedroom door behind her.

Should she go talk to her mom? *No, Dad is waiting. I'll call her tomorrow.* Melena ran back upstairs and into her room. She glanced around and smiled. Ten months without Cassi. "Yes!" *Not a minute too soon.* She picked up the last two boxes and pranced down the stairs, ready for the blessed change.

A soft wail came from the back of the house. It sounded like her mom. Melena pinched her lips together and sighed. She walked back out to her dad. "Dad, I need to talk to Mom for a second. Do we have time?"

He glanced at his watch. "Yeah, go ahead."

She ran back inside to her mother's door and knocked.

There was a hesitant response. "Come in."

Melena pushed the door open and found her mother trying to sit up. The tear-mixed mascara streamed down her cheeks, smearing her usually perfect face. Her nose was red to match her blood-shot eyes. Melena didn't know what to think. She'd never seen her mother show any emotion, let alone breakdown. She shifted forward, leery of the wrong reaction.

"Mom, are you okay?"

She pointed at a box of tissues on the dresser. "Can you hand that to me?"

Melena passed the box across the bed and perched on the edge of the mattress. "Do you want to talk about it?"

Her mom tossed her head back and dabbed at her eyes. "What's that, dear?"

"Why you're crying? Is Brian leaving you?"

Her mother pulled the tissue back from her eyes and glared at her. "Don't you need to be going? Your dad is here."

"Mom, I just thought..." Melena reached out to touch her shoulder.

Her mom recoiled. "Don't keep him waiting. You know how he can be." Her mom shifted off the bed, walked in the bathroom, and shut the door.

Melena sat in a daze, staring at her mother's exit. *Why is it so hard for Mom to open up?* The ache squeezed her heart. Melena fought the tears threatening to fall. She glanced around the white room. Unlike her friends' homes, not one family picture hung in this home. Instead expensive paintings and sculptures filled the empty space.

Cassi swung the door open and sauntered in holding an ice bag. She glanced over at Melena. "Mom?"

"She's in the bathroom." Melena nodded to the closed door. "But I think she wants to be left alone."

Cassi rolled her eyes, crossed to the door, and knocked. "Mom, it's me, Cassi."

"Come in, dear."

She cracked the door open and peered in. "You all right?"

"No, not really. Come in and shut the door, okay?"

Salt poured in Melena's wounded heart. She rose from the bed and lagged to the door. *Mom's right. I need to go.*

Chapter Fourteen

A little before eleven, Melena and her father arrived at the four-bedroom condo in Fullerton. She'd never been so happy to see a building in her life. She walked in the living room and breathed in the smell of Old Spice. She glanced around the living room and simpered. The brown futon was covered in newspapers, an open soda can rested on the pine coffee table without a coaster, and in the corner, the Indian rug was curled on one end. *Disorder. I love it and am so happy to be home.*

Melena followed her dad into her room. He set the boxes down and went back outside. She dropped her suitcase on the bed and moved to the door. Her dad walked in with the rest of the boxes and placed them with the others.

"Why don't you unpack tomorrow? I'll make us a snack and then you can get some rest."

She threw her arms around his neck and smiled. "I'm so glad to be back home, Dad."

He hugged her tight, then untangled from her arms. "Come on, let's find something in the kitchen worth eating."

They rummaged through the cupboards and the refrigerator, deciding on English muffin pizzas made with spaghetti sauce, ham, and string cheese.

"Always the amazing chef," Melena said, threading

a strand of cheese into her mouth.

"Maybe I should have done that rather than become a preacher, huh?" He licked some stray sauce from his lip.

Melena laughed. "Hey, we all have our calling."

He slapped her leg and smiled. "Okay, now that I've fed you, why don't you tell me what's been going on with you and your sister. Nick isn't one for details, just enraged emotion."

She slid the empty paper plate on the coffee table and relaxed on the futon. *Where to begin?* She stared at her dad. His once brown hair and beard now held streaks of gray. His eyes crinkled at the edges of his almond-shaped, green-hazel eyes. How she'd missed him this summer. They'd always been close. He was a wonderful father and a great spiritual leader. She valued his opinion. With a big breath, she told him everything that had happened—from youth camp to the present. He listened quietly with a stoic expression, nodding when appropriate. She could tell little what he was thinking by his posture. "So, there is my wonderful summer in a nutshell."

He crossed his arms, took a deep breath, and leaned back. A familiar pose. It usually meant he had something important to say.

She shifted.

"I'm sorry about your sister. Sounds to me like this whole thing can be solved by finding out what your sister has done."

"I know, but how? When Dylan called, he acted like I was a total stranger. I must have done something really bad."

"You mean Cassi has probably done something

really bad." He rubbed his hairy chin. "She really could have used more discipline, but you know how your mom is. When Cassi was at her house, she could do whatever she wanted and I suppose she still does."

"Did you know she wasn't going to stay with you this year?"

He frowned. "Yeah, she called me last week."

"What did she say?"

"That she didn't want to live with a religious fanatic anymore." His voice cracked and he blinked back the tears in his eyes.

"Oh, Dad, I'm sorry." He was an amazing man and didn't deserve this. It broke her heart.

"Yeah, well, your mother's hogwash has finally been digested." His expression softened. "You can't hate her, Melena. You need to learn to pray for her. Like the Bible says, 'Love your enemies and pray for those who hurt you…do good to those who hate you.'"

"Yeah, it's the mantra I say at least once a day, but it's so hard." Her eyes welled up and she looked up to keep the tears from falling.

Her dad got up from his chair and sat next to her. "I know it hurts. Please try to understand why she acts this way." He sighed. "When I look at Cassandra, I don't see an evil girl. I see a starving soul."

Melena nodded and grinned. "Yeah."

He cleared his throat. "So, what else?"

She shrugged and exhaled through her nose. Grateful for a new topic. "Um…do you think you could take me to pick up my dress tomorrow?"

"Dress?"

"For the end-of-the-summer banquet."

"Sure, but I thought…"

The front knob turned and Nick entered. "Melena, welcome home, sis."

She leapt from the couch and flew into his arms. He grabbed her and swung her around. Then grabbed her from around the back and playfully rubbed his knuckle across her skull. His famous noogie. He used to give them to her all the time when they were kids. She pushed away laughing. "Stop!" She smoothed her disheveled hair. "You call that a welcome?"

He grinned. "I most certainly do."

Melena rolled her eyes and flopped back on the couch.

"A little late to be up, don't you think?"

Melena dipped an eyebrow. "You should talk since it's after midnight."

"Some of us work for a living." He pulled off his coat and tossed it at the couch, half of it landing on Melena's head.

"Thanks." She sputtered and tossed it off onto the floor. "I'm going to get a job after I figure out my schedule with school and volleyball."

"You're nineteen in six months. You can't live with your parents forever."

She tossed a pillow at him. He ducked just in time.

Their dad stretched and rose from the chair. "Well, children, I've had enough. I'm going to bed."

Melena got up and kissed his cheek. "Night, Dad."

"Night, sweetheart. You're going to be okay."

"Thanks, Dad."

He hugged Nick and went to his room.

Nick sat on the floor across from her. "So, what's new with you?"

She considered mentioning Brian leaving, but

wasn't in the mood for another emotional conversation, so she decided to save it for later. "Did you hear I made Spikers?"

"Of course, who hasn't? I'm pretty sure it was on the news and Oprah called earlier. How does August 20 look for you?"

She shook her head. "My brother, the comedian. So, what's up with you?"

He pulled his legs up and rested his wrists on his knees. "Hmm? I'm seeing someone."

Melena leaned forward and gasped. "No way! Who?"

A sly smiled crossed his face and he looked away with the famous Harrison blush.

She dropped to her knees and crawled to his side. "Come on. You can't drop a bomb like that and not ante up. Who is she?" Her brother had promised at a *True Love Waits* seminar years ago to not only stay pure until marriage, but also to only date a potential mate. If he was dating someone, she'd have to be special.

"Okay, promise you won't laugh."

She pinched her lips together and mumbled, "Promise."

He took a deep breath. "Sherry."

"Sherry?" Didn't ring any bells.

"Sherry Park."

"Sherry Park." Melena repeated, afraid she heard correctly. "*The* Sherry Park?"

He nodded.

"The girl guys used to call 'Park Bench' and chant 'Sherry's so very, very'?"

He grimaced. "Yeah."

"Wow." She pinched her lips together. *What can I*

say? The girl had been made fun of almost every day of her adolescent life. In tenth grade, she had tried to commit suicide. When she returned to school, the hazing got worse. People openly threw things at her, tagged her locker, and destroyed her personal property. Eventually, she was pulled out to home school.

"She's not what you think, Mel."

"What do I think?"

"That she's a fat girl who tried to kill herself."

Once again, what could Melena say? She threw her head back and sighed. "Do you like her?"

"I may love her."

The words went off like a bomb in the room. Melena didn't respond right away. She studied her brother's face. He seemed happy. That was enough. She shrugged. "Then who cares what I think?"

He narrowed his eyes. "You and I are best friends. We don't do that."

"I know, but it's true." She squared her shoulders. "So, tell me how you two met?"

He leaned his back against the recliner and yawned.

Melena couldn't help but follow suit. She yawned, too. "Don't do that. I'm exhausted."

"Sorry." He smiled. "I was failing calculus last year and needed a tutor. Principal Robson suggested her."

"But she doesn't go to school, right?"

"Actually, her name is still on the roster. She just doesn't attend classes." He flapped his hand in the air. "Anyway, I called her and we met every Monday after school for the whole year. She's got the funniest sense of humor. It's dry, and you have to be paying attention, but it's hilarious."

She watched his expression. Nick's eyes lit up as he talked about her.

"She's really pretty. I know people look at her and just see an overweight girl. But I don't. I see this amazing, beautiful human being."

Awe, Nick. She always knew her brother was a great guy. "So, you two are serious?"

A big smile spread cheek to cheek. "Yeah, she's the one."

Melena's heart skipped. She touched his hand. "I'm so happy for you."

"Do you think it would be okay if I brought her to the banquet? I know I haven't been to Faith Community in a while, but I want to do something special with her."

She gave him a sideways glance. "Nick, you've gone to that church more than I have. You spent all last year down south. I just attend during the summer."

"Good point. I'll call in the morning."

She yawned again. "Okay, that's it. I'm going to bed. We can talk more tomorrow."

He stood and helped her up. "Are you okay? I mean, after everything you said the other day?"

She sighed. "I would be if I could find peace in the whole Cassi-Dylan thing. It just weighs on me, you know?"

He wrapped his arm around her shoulders and squeezed. "Yeah."

"Good night, Nick."

He let her go. "See you tomorrow."

She walked to her room and closed the door. The thought of Nick and Sherry together made her smile, then cry. He was two and a half years younger than her, and he had found his soul mate.

Why am I so hung up on Dylan? I knew him for what? A few days. But she knew the answer. She had never felt so connected to another human being. She pulled off her clothes and stepped into a pair of sweats and a T-shirt. Climbing into bed, she began to pray.

Lord, I'm tired of feeling this pain. I'm sick of all the bitterness. The hurt. I would love nothing more than to work things out with Dylan, but more than that, I need to work things out with Cassi. I need peace.

Chapter Fifteen

Melena peeked through the cracks in her lids. *Where am I?* She blinked to clear her vision. A peace washed over her. The walls were burgundy red with ink drawings. Her vestibule was decorated with her childhood china-doll collection and positioned in the corner was an ebony changing screen. Her heart soared. *I'm home.*

There was a light knock.

"Yes?"

"Can I come in?" Nick said.

"By all means." She sat up against the black headboard.

"Did you get a good night's sleep?"

"Yeah, for once, I didn't have to listen to Cassi's snoring."

"Hey, that's what I wanted to talk to you about."

"Cassi's snoring?"

He chuckled. "No." He sat on the edge of her bed and looked in her eyes. "Mel, do you remember when you were six years old and you found out Mom was having a baby girl? Someone besides your dumb baby brother to play with?"

"Dumb baby brother?" She hit his arm. "Yeah, I remember."

"But in the long run, you decided you liked playing with your little brother more, because he was easier to

153

get along with."

"Yeah?"

"Well, I just wanted to remind you nothing has changed. You have managed to get along without Cassi's friendship your whole life. Don't let her get you down now. If you really like Dylan, then I'll try and find out what happened."

"Thanks."

"But what about Rick?"

"What about him?" She shrugged. "We're going to the banquet together."

"I heard you are a couple now."

She pushed her head back. "I don't think so."

He furrowed his brow. "You don't *think* so?"

"Well, he's a real nice guy…"

"And?"

She picked at the ties on the quilt. "I'd probably be better off with him…"

"But?"

She sighed. "But I don't really like him that way. He's just a friend."

Nick slapped her thigh. "Good."

"Good?" Her lips tugged downward. "What do you mean good? I thought you wanted us together."

"No, I want you to be happy. I don't want to waste my time trying to fix your relationship with Dylan, if you're still hung up on Rick."

She laughed. "Understood."

"However, I don't know if I really want you to go out with someone who hangs out with Cassi. It doesn't really say much about his character."

"Why does everyone have to keep pointing that out?"

Nick shrugged. "Because it's an obvious concern."

"Yeah, I've thought about that and I think I have the answer." She crossed her legs and leaned her elbows on her knees. "Dating Cassi would be the greatest revenge."

"That doesn't say much for his character either."

She rolled her eyes. "He's a good guy, Nick. Just bewitched somehow."

He nodded, then stood. "Well, if you're still planning to go to the mall, you'd better get dressed."

"The mall?"

"April has your car and Dad said you wanted to pick up your dress."

"Oh, you're right." She hopped out of bed and reached for the robe just inside her closet door. "Just let me get a quick shower, okay?"

"I'll fix you some breakfast."

She spun around. "Breakfast?"

"A welcome back breakfast, but don't count on it becoming a new Harrison tradition." He grinned and closed the door.

She smiled. *Yes, it is good to be home.*

****

There was a knock at the door. Dylan slipped on a pair of board shorts and grabbed the first T-shirt he saw. Peering through the hole, he cringed. *Cassi. What does she want?* She'd been calling all week. So far, he had succeeded in avoiding her. He pulled the top over his head, unlocked the latch on the door, and peeked out. "Cassi, it's early. What do you want?"

Her lip protruded forward in a pout. "Don't be mad. You said you'd go to the banquet with me, so I thought maybe we could talk over the details. I've been calling all week."

I know. He resisted the urge to roll his eyes.

"So, is it cool?"

"Is what cool?"

"That I come in so we can talk?"

He let out an exaggerated sigh. "I'm going out with Chad. We can only talk for a few minutes."

She sauntered to the couch and flopped down. "So, I was thinking red."

****

Nick slid a plate of bacon and over-easy eggs across the counter. "I know how you eat at Mom's, but no yogurt today. We're celebrating your return."

"What's going on here?" Dad said, walking through the kitchen doorway. "Who made breakfast?"

"I'm spoiling my sister which won't happen again." Nick smiled.

"Any left for your old man?" He straddled a stool at the end of the counter and leaned forward.

Melena poured him a cup of coffee, while Nick fixed a plate.

"If all fathers could be as lucky as I am..." He nipped off a bite of bacon and grinned.

Melena gazed from her dad to her brother, then began to hum.

"Well, somebody's in a better mood this morning," her father said.

"Yeah, I guess I am." She cut into her egg and watched the yoke spill out. Her stomach wrenched. It had been a while since she'd allowed herself to eat a decent meal. She broke off a piece of bacon, wrapped it in egg, and brought it to her mouth. *Mmm.* "Thanks for doing this, Nick."

"Ah, sure." He sat across from her with an egg sandwich piled high with lots of bacon and yoke dripping from the bread.

"I'm just happy to be back to sanity."

"Well, I'm glad you're back," her dad said. "I hate when you're gone."

She touched her father's hand. "I missed you, too." She took another bite and washed it down with orange juice. Ease filled her being. *Why'd I ever leave Dad's house?* It was where she belonged. "I don't think I'm going back to Mom's next year."

Her father looked up from his plate. "Really?"

"I'm an adult now and I don't really see the point." She scraped her fork on her plate to pick up the little pieces of egg left. "That way I can see Kevin and..."

"Avoid Cassi," Nick said.

She smirked. "Precisely."

Nick cleared his throat. "Well, I'll back you up, no matter what you decide."

"There's more."

Her father laid his fork down and wiped his mouth. "Oh?"

"Brian left Mom."

Nick raised an eyebrow. Her dad just looked at his coffee cup.

"When?" Nick said.

"I don't know exactly, but Mom was pretty broken up yesterday."

Nick shook his head. "Mom crying? That I'd like to see."

Melena stood and walked to the sink with her plate. "No, you don't. It wasn't pretty."

"No, I don't suppose I would."

Melena rinsed her plate and placed it in the dishwasher. The air was thick and her dad wasn't responding. "So, Dad, how's the mission project going?"

He looked up, startled. "Huh? Oh, good. You should come out and help us." He wiped his hands with a napkin and pushed his plate away. "Unless you plan to get a job."

Her father had started an organization to help missionary children cope when coming home from the mission field. He helped the older ones write resumes, get jobs, and learn about culture and social norms. Though he started out of his home, the need was overwhelming. He now had to enlist help throughout the country.

Nick stretched and pushed himself up. "You about ready to go?" He grabbed the truck keys from the counter and dangled them in the air.

Their father lowered his coffee cup and swallowed. "Are you two going somewhere?"

"Remember, Melena has to pick up her dress at the mall."

"That's right." He set his cup down. "I meant to ask you about that last night. I thought Dylan wasn't going to take you."

"Rick is taking me."

He raised an eyebrow. "Well, if you're with Rick, why are you so upset about Dylan?"

She grinned. "Rick and I are just friends, Dad. He knows all about Dylan." It was the truth although she knew Rick wanted more. A pang of guilt reared, but she quickly pushed the feeling aside. *I have to be at the banquet. I have to see Dylan one more time.* If her dad knew what she was thinking, he'd be disappointed. She gave him a hug and said "good-bye" before she felt any worse.

Melena opened the door to her brother's truck and turned her nose up at the interior. The seat was covered in CDs, a beach towel, and fast food containers. Granules of sand covered the floorboard, along with surf magazines and empty energy-drink cans.

"Nice car, Nick."

He leaned through the driver's side and scooped some of it behind his seat. "Sorry. I've been going from work to the beach a lot." He sat in his seat and slammed his door.

Melena scraped at the stray fries and sand. "You might want to clean it out before the banquet. I don't think Sherry is going to want to ride in this mess." She ventured into the seat and closed her door, kicking the cans at her feet.

"Don't worry, I've got it covered."

Melena stared out the window on the way to the mall. The sun was high and bright, promising to be a scorcher. The dry Santa Ana winds were finally gone and the horrid humidity had returned. She had forced Dylan out of her mind as much as possible, but going to get her dress made his absence that much more real. She just hoped he showed at the banquet. Maybe they could talk then. Well, that is if she could pull him away from Cassi. If for nothing else but to ask him why? Why he led Melena on, only to hook up with her biggest enemy?

Within twenty minutes, they pulled into the mall. Nick got lucky and found a spot near the front. They crossed the walkway and he opened the mall door.

Melena stepped in and sighed. The cool air caressed her skin. "It feels good in here."

Nick nodded. "So, where did you buy your dress?"

"Vogue Venture. It's on the west end by JCPenney's."

"Here it is," she said. On her way to the counter, she paused to admire a slender mannequin dressed in a see-through blue gown, leaning against a silver disco ball and holding a champagne glass in her right hand. "That's pretty."

"Come on. We aren't here to look, we're here to buy." He pushed her to the counter. "Besides, Dad would never let you wear that farther than the bathroom."

She giggled. "Don't worry. I'm nothing more than a window shopper. I'm not Mom."

The saleslady took the time to neatly wrap the dress in a blue and silver box that matched the front display. She tied a silver bow on the box that read, "Thank you for shopping with us."

Melena paid, gathered her package, and left the store with Nick in tow. Without much thought, she headed for the parking garage.

"Where are you going?" Nick grabbed her arm. "Don't you want to grab some ice-cream or something? I mean, we drove twenty minutes to get here. It would be a shame to just pick up your dress and go home."

"I'm really not in the mood to run into anyone right now." *A certain someone to be exact.*

"Look, I could have gone to the beach today with my friends, but no, I sacrificed my time to spend the day with my favorite sister. I don't want to go yet. You can go sit in the car if you want, but I am getting some ice-cream." He offered her a tight smile and walked to Yogurt Chip a few feet away.

Fine. Just don't let anyone be here. All she wanted to do was go home and think about Dylan while drowning her sorrows in sugar. Ice cream would do, but she wanted it at home.

She ordered a peanut butter yogurt with carob chips and joined her brother at a table in the middle of the food court. To her misfortune, the mall was raining friends, enemies, and acquaintances at every corner. Melena tried to be polite, but knew she was failing.

Nick eyed her, obviously uncomfortable with her sudden rudeness. "Okay, what's your deal? You've just about snubbed half of your graduating class."

She shrugged and licked a carob chip from her spoon. "I told you I didn't want to talk to anyone, didn't I? You're the one who insisted I come and get ice cream."

"Okay, Cassi."

She glared at him. "That's not fair, Nick."

"Well, you're acting like her."

Maybe she was being rude—but being compared to Cassi—that stung. Tears pressed against her lashes. She snatched a napkin from the holder and dabbed at her eyes. *What is wrong with me? I should be over this by now. Why do I have to be such a girl? Get a grip.*

"Melena, I'm sorry. I didn't mean it." He reached to take her free hand, but she withdrew it.

"Look, I know." She sniffed. "I'm just so confused and you being mad at me doesn't help." She buried her head in her hands. It wasn't just about Dylan anymore. It was about Cassi and how she could be evil enough to take her boyfriend. "I don't know what to do."

"I told you. I will talk to him, okay?"

"No, I meant about Cassi." She lifted her head. "The more she enters my mind, the more I loathe her. Dad, the pastor, everybody says I'm supposed to love her and I made a vow at camp to try. But honestly, I don't know how." She swiped at her eyes. "What kind of person hates their own sister?"

He pulled another napkin from the holder and placed it in her open hand. "You're not near Cassi anymore. Try not to think about her."

"Ugh! Trust me, I've tried. Can't you see that everything I do, she tries to destroy? As always, she took the one thing that meant something to me and made it hers. She even got Mom to trust her."

"She didn't take everything that matters to you. You still have Dad, me, and your relationship with God." He scooped a spoonful of fudge yogurt on the spoon and brought it to his mouth. "And volleyball. She didn't even make the cut."

Melena hid her smile behind a napkin. "Really?"

"Really." He folded his hands on the table and bent forward. "Personally, I think what you're upset about is Dylan, not Cassi."

She stared at the soupy liquid in her cup and tried to block the queasiness that always followed the current topic. "I'm trying to put him out of my mind. I can't deal with him anymore. Cassi is the root of everything wrong in my life."

"If Dylan were to come here and take you into the sunset, you'd forget Cassi without hesitation. So, I still say it's Dylan."

She stared at her brother. *Do I hit him or hug him?* He always tried to push her to admit things she didn't want to admit. When they were kids, he got her to confess all sorts of things to their dad. He said his job was to make sure she turned out okay. Forgetting the fact he's the younger brother. *Whatever.* "Okay, I relent. It's Dylan, but it's Cassi, too."

"So, get rid of Cassi and everything will be better." He scraped the bottom of his cup and glanced up with a smirk.

"Get rid of Cassi? She's your sister, too."

He shrugged. "I'm not getting rid of her. You are."

She laughed. "You're crazy, you know that? Besides, that's not the right thing to do and you know it."

"Who is lecturing who here?" Nick laughed.

"Well, your advice stinks." She smiled. "Get rid of Cassi. I'm so sure."

He stood over the table and pulled her down to give her a noogie.

"Uncle!" She pushed away, straightening her hair.

Nick's cell phone rang in his pocket. He pulled it out, read the screen, and then answered it. "Hello?" He smiled. "Hi, Sherry. Yeah, give me a half-hour. I love you, too. Okay, bye." He ended the call with a punch of the button. "Thanks to my girlfriend, I'm going to make your day." He stood and tossed his cup in the trash. "Let's get out of here."

Chapter Sixteen

Later that afternoon, Melena opened the door to April, who stood on the doorstep loaded down with her belongings.

"No way. Your mom said yes?" Melena said, taking a duffel bag from April's arms.

She nodded and dragged two suitcases behind her. "I'm here until school starts in September."

"Cool!" Melena couldn't have been happier. She needed her best friend now more than ever. "This is going to be so fun."

April dropped her stuff on the guest room floor and threw her hands palm out in front of her. "I know. How fetch is this?"

Melena rushed into her friend's arms.

April and she fell backward on the bed, then rolled onto the floor. April snorted and the two women doubled over laughing.

When she caught her breath, Melena said, "Yes, this is going to be a blast." She unzipped a duffel bag on the bed and pulled out a stack of April's clothes. "Might as well get you unpacked." As she stuffed jeans in the top drawer of the dresser, her stomach flipped. She'd been dying to ask April about Dylan. *Do I ask? April might get mad.* Melena pressed her lips together and took a deep breath through her nose. *Just ask. Keep it casual.* "So, last night…"

April glanced at her and popped her gum. "Yes?"

"You went to that pool party at Chad's house. Did you happen to see Dylan there?"

"Still hung up on him, huh?"

Melena didn't answer, just studied a pile of shoes in one of the bags.

April turned away from the dresses she had just hung in the closet and shook her head. "Dylan showed up for about ten minutes, then took off. Cassi wasn't there. At least, not that I saw." She folded her hands and stepped closer with a serious expression. "But I do have something to tell you not related? Kind of my own issue."

Melena let go of the shoes in her hand and faced her. "What?"

"Chad asked me to the summer banquet?"

Melena grinned. "And? Did you say yes?"

A smile broke across her face. "Of course. I mean, Seth won't be down for one more week, and I figured since he won't be here to take me it would be okay to go with Chad. Don't you agree?" April plopped back on the bed, her eyes pleading for a positive response.

Melena bit her bottom lip and sank down next to her. "I like the idea of Chad and you together, but I don't know, April. If you lead Chad on, you could end up hurting him when Seth returns." She touched her friend's hand. "Or vice versa."

"I've been going surfing with Chad almost every morning and when I'm not working or with you, we've been hanging out." April grabbed a tissue from the end table and wrapped her gum inside. "I think I'm falling in love with him."

"Seriously?"

April wilted back on the bed and tried to conceal her face with a red throw pillow. "Yeah, seriously."

Melena tried to pull the pillow away. "I told you this long-distance romance stuff would never work out."

"I know, I know." She rolled over and sat up flinging her hands dramatically to the bed. "Seth is moving here to be near me. Help!"

Melena chuckled. "Okay, now you sound like me. You must be desperate if you want *my* help."

She met her eyes. "I am desperate."

Melena couldn't remember a time when April had been desperate for anyone or anything. She always seemed in control, annoyingly so. Helping April dispersed some of Melena's heartache for the moment. She folded her legs and faced her. "Okay, look. You've been with Seth for over two years, right?"

April nodded.

"As far as I know, he's always been good to you?"

She nodded again.

"And you still love him?"

April shrugged. "Of course."

"Then why would you want to ruin a perfectly good relationship?"

Her eyes went wide. "Melena!"

"What?"

"Hello? Listen to your own advice. You're going out with Enrique, when you really want Dylan." She crossed her arms and pushed back to the headboard. "Have you thought for a moment about how you might hurt Enrique's feelings?"

"Rick and I are just friends."

April touched her shoulder. "He might just be *your*

friend, but I saw him the other day. You thought I went straight to the car, but I watched you two. I assure you, he has a different relationship in mind."

"Maybe that's true. But I don't like him like that. He held my hand at the mall and I felt nothing. No zing."

"Really, no zing." April laughed. "I can't believe you didn't tell me he held your hand."

Melena bit her fingernail and smiled sheepishly. "Um…actually, he kissed me."

"What?" April slapped Melena's foot. "Jerk! I'm your best friend. You're supposed to tell me those things."

"Sorry. It's just so frustrating, you know." She flopped back on the twin bed, almost knocking April on the floor.

"Watch it!" April kicked her playfully.

"Sorry." Melena grinned, then sighed. "So, what am I supposed to do?"

"Well, I like Chad and Seth. What do I do? Encourage Chad and hurt Seth? Or forget Chad and hurt him?"

"Men!" They said in unison, then started laughing.

April pulled her legs up and rested her chin on her knees. "The truth is I'm tired of dating Seth. He's the only guy I've ever dated. If I don't break it off soon, I'll probably end up marrying him."

"Would that be so bad? I've only met him once, but he seems like a good guy."

April sighed. "I'm eighteen, Melena. I'm way too young to be tied down to one man. College, missions, work—I've got dreams."

"Then tell him that. Tell him you need to take a

break. If he loves you, he'll wait."

She pouted. "Yeah, but he's moving out here for me."

"No." A grin slowly spread across Melena's face. "He's moving to San Diego to enlist in the Navy. Remember?"

The light went on in April's eyes. "That's right." She grinned. "Problem solved."

Melena frowned. "I'm glad yours is."

April scooted next to her and wrapped an arm around her shoulders. "Hey, it'll work out. God is in control."

Every time Melena thought she could block out her feelings, they slapped her in the face. She really needed some time in prayer. When was the last time she journaled or read her Bible? *No wonder I'm a mess.*

"Do you mind if I let you finish unpacking? I want to go sit out on the porch and pray for a while."

"Are you okay?"

"I'm fine." Okay, so that was a lie. She was far from fine, but that was why she needed some time alone.

"Okay."

Melena retrieved her Bible and journal from her room, then walked to the kitchen, grabbed a soda, and sauntered onto the first floor balcony. She sat on a lawn chair and faced the street. Few cars were visible from the condo, but the city buzzed with life. In the distance, she could see the man-made white mountain—the Matterhorn roller coaster. Throughout the year, she and her father spent evenings watching the fireworks from Disneyland. *I wonder if they'll be shooting off any tonight.* She popped the ring on her can and sighed. She took a swig, then set it down, and opened her Bible.

She flipped over to the New Testament and landed on 1 Corinthians 13:2: *"I can have all the ministry in the world, but if I have not love, I am nothing."*

Great. Love. Not encouraging. A hard concept to grasp when there were three people in her life who seemed either incapable or unwilling to love her back. *God help me to be stronger.* She flipped over to the Old Testament and landed on Zechariah 13. She stopped and re-read verse nine: *"I will bring into the fire...refine them like silver and test them like gold. They will call on My name and I will answer them."*

A tear slid down her cheek. She wiped it on her arm, then opened her journal, and wrote:

August 10

You hear the cry of my heart and now is my testing time. You are molding me and preparing me for Your will. I praise you, Lord, for already you are at work in my life. I pray for Cassi and her heart. Only you can truly break through that barrier. And if there is anything in me that is wrong, let me make it right.

She started to write more when she caught a movement out of the corner of her eye. She looked up.

Enrique sauntered up the walkway in loose jeans and a striped tee. His hair hung loose around his shoulders and something heavy weighed in his eyes. "Hey there," he said as he approached the steps.

Jesus, help me now. She forced a smile. "Hey, Rick."

"I hope I'm not catching you at a bad time."

She shook her head and set her journal on the ground. "No, not at all."

"Great." He grabbed hold of the railing and

boosted himself up and over.

Her stomach hurt with anxiety. She wasn't ready to tell him the truth. *Keep it light.* "How's it going?"

"Okay. Just came from the library. Trying to find a book for my class. No such luck."

She raised an eyebrow. "You're still taking classes?"

He nodded. "Last one. English 210."

"What book is it?"

"Asher Lev."

"Oh, I have it from class with Mr. Stepka. You're welcome to borrow it."

He clapped his hands together. "Yeah, that would be great."

She stood and grabbed the screen door handle. "I'll go grab it."

He shook his head. "I can get it from you later. I don't really need it for a few more weeks."

"Are you sure? Because I know right where it is." She pointed with her thumb over her shoulder. Secretly, she wanted to tell April he was here. Maybe with a third party, things were less likely to get uncomfortable.

"No, I only have a few minutes before I'm supposed to go to work." He leaned against the railing and crossed his arms. "I need to ask you something, and I want you to be honest with me, okay?"

Her pulse quickened. Here it came. "Sure."

Pain bore in his eyes. *Okay, I'm a big jerk.* Whether or not she was ready, she had to tell him the truth. Dylan didn't love her, but Rick might. *Heart, why won't you cooperate? He's nice, he's good looking, and I've liked him for years. What is my problem? Ah!*

"This whole date thing isn't real. You're not really

into me, are you?"

She glanced away. "I'm sorry, Rick. I want to be and I'm trying."

His jaw tightened. "No, please don't *try*. I don't want to be a consolation prize for any girl."

"I don't want it to be like that." She met his gaze and stepped closer to him. "I really don't want to hurt you."

His expression softened. "It's okay." He reached out a thumb and touched her cheek. "You still like him, don't you?"

"Yes," she whispered, her voice hoarse.

"I can't believe I'm going to say this." He took a breath. "I went down to La Jolla Shores the other day to meet up with some guys in my surf club. While I was down there, I ran into your sister. She was hanging on this guy."

Melena sighed. "Dylan."

"Yeah, but I got the impression he didn't really like Cassi. He was there to surf with some of his buddies, she acted like a groupie." He glanced down at his watch. "Actually, I'm pretty sure he still likes you."

She looked up, stunned. *How could he know that?* Her mouth hung open as she tried to digest his words. "What makes you say that? He avoids me like the plague. If he cared, he wouldn't hurt me by ignoring me."

Enrique shifted from one foot to the other. "I didn't realize who he was at first. I mentioned to Cassi that you and I were going to the banquet together and he got mad."

Her heart started to beat again. "Mad? At you?"

He nodded. "Yeah. He didn't say anything. Just

shook his head, grabbed his board, and ran into the ocean."

"And Cassi?"

"They really didn't seem like they were a couple. He never held her hand or anything. She followed him around, but he seemed indifferent."

Melena blinked. "Why are you helping me?"

He stepped forward and touched her chin. "Because we've been friends for a long time, and I care about you. I'm tired of seeing you unhappy." He kissed her cheek and smiled. "If Dylan is what will make you happy, then I want you to have a chance with him."

The pressure of tears caught in her throat. She swallowed. "Do you still want to go to the banquet with me?"

"The chance to see you in that dress again?" He smiled. "Absolutely." He gave her a hug.

He understands. The weight of bricks fell off her back. "Rick, you know I had a mad crush on you for years."

"Yeah, and my timing is perfect."

She half-grinned. "Why am I stupid enough to let a guy like you go?"

He stepped back. "Beats me."

"I hope you know…" She offered a grin. "That I really do care about you."

His eyes lingered on hers for a moment, then he abruptly broke away and jammed his hands in his pockets. "Well, I'd better go. I'll see you Friday." He sat back on the railing, spun around, and jumped to the ground. "Bye."

She waved as he disappeared around the corner. Melena swung open the screen door and yelled, "April?

April, where are you?"

"In the bathroom."

Melena slid across the tile floor in her socks and halted in front of the door. "You're never going to believe what just happened?"

April flipped off the light and joined her in the hall. "Rick was here."

Melena furrowed her eyebrows. "How'd you know?"

"I saw him leave."

Melena batted at the air. "Well, he understands everything and..." She grabbed April's shoulders and beamed.

"And?"

"Dylan got mad when he found out Rick was taking me to the banquet."

April crossed her arms and scowled. "He doesn't have the right to get mad. Jerk! He's with Cassi."

Melena let go and paced back. "Don't call him a jerk."

April shrugged. "Sorry, but if he's with Cassi, he's a—"

"That's just it. Rick said Dylan didn't really seem interested in Cassi. That she was more with him than the other way around."

"Cassi has tricked him somehow." April walked into the kitchen, reached for a banana, peeled it, and took a bite. "And I intend to find out how."

Melena was tired of being a mouse. She wanted answers. If she had to be miserable at least, she deserved to know why. "You still want to go to that party at Kelly's house?"

April gave her a sideways glance. "I thought you

didn't want to go."

"You invited Chad?"

A slow smile crept on her face. "Yes, I did."

"Then let's do it. Let's go."

****

"Hey, there you are, man," Chad said, walking into the carport. "You up to another swim party?"

Dylan started to answer, when a car pulled alongside them. Cassi got out of the passenger side and waved. "Thanks, Beth." He blushed at the sight of her. She wore white short shorts and a pink mid-drift tee. Her black bikini was visible from all angles.

"Hey, guys." She sauntered up alongside Dylan. "Rumor has it there is a rave up north at that Kelly girl's house."

Chad crossed his arms and faced her. "How would you know?"

"I have my sources."

Dylan dumped the hose back on the cement and screwed the water off. "I'm washing my surf equipment. You guys have fun."

Chad stepped next to him and whispered. "She's right. It's a great party. April invited us to go."

Dylan hung his wetsuit on top of his surfboard and looked at him. April possibly meant Melena. "We don't even know Kelly."

He shrugged. "Who cares? We know April and Melena."

Cassi folded her arms in a huff. "Not her again."

Dylan cocked his head to the side and stared at Cassi. *What a brat!* Did he go and risk running into Melena? Did he not go and miss the chance to run into her? Why couldn't he just let her go? "It's probably all the way up in Orange County, right?"

"Kind of. I guess Kelly lives in San Juan Capistrano. It's like halfway." He slapped Dylan's bare stomach with the back of his hand. "Forty minutes tops and you're already dressed."

Dylan glanced down. He only had on blue board shorts. "I was going job hunting this afternoon."

Chad shook his head. "You did that yesterday. Not a bite. Come on. There's always tomorrow."

Dylan wiped his hands on his shorts. He didn't feel like going anywhere, let alone somewhere that could end in disaster. "Is that Enrique guy going to be there?"

"I don't know. You want me to call April and ask?"

Dylan looked from his friend to Cassi. Her ride left, so he'd probably have to take her with him. That would go over well if he saw Melena. But then, maybe that was okay too. Melena had obviously moved on. Closure is what he needed. Maybe seeing her again would offer that. "Fine, give me a second."

****

April and Melena arrived at Kelly's swim party a little late. They knocked on the door and Kelly answered. "Hey, I'm glad you made it. Come on in." She stepped out of the way. "Everyone is outside on the patio."

April and Melena walked through the living room and out the sliding glass door.

"Is Keith here?" Melena said, holding up a plastic bag. "Nick wanted me to give him something."

"Yeah, he's over by the table of food in the corner." She pointed across the cemented back yard. "I'm keeping him busy as the official hot dog gourmet."

"Thanks." The two girls waded their way through an onslaught of young people talking and eating, past an overflowing Jacuzzi, to where Keith stood drinking a soda. Melena stopped a few feet in front of the pool.

April ran into the back of her, almost giving her friend a dip. "Melena? What's wrong with you?"

"They're here," Melena hissed.

She followed her gaze. Dylan and Cassi sat in the shallow end of the pool with Chad and another guy. It was the first time she'd seen Dylan since the mess began. Her lungs gasped for air. "I think I'm going to faint."

April held one of Melena's wrists. "Maybe you should sit."

Ignoring her, Melena kept her eyes on Dylan. He looked amazing. Small drops of water beaded on his tan taut muscles and rippled chest, glistening in the sun. His wet lashes made his dark eyes intense. Her heart accelerated. He laughed with Chad, until he caught Melena's eye.

Her heart shot blood rapidly into her head. Stars flashed in front of her face. She willed herself to stay upright.

He held her gaze for a second, then turned away, his smile gone.

She grabbed April's arm and dragged her to the food table. "Why is Cassi here?"

Keith walked up between them holding a pair of hotdogs in tongs. "Anyone hungry?"

Melena held up her hand. "No, thanks." Then held out the plastic bag. "Here."

"Hi, Keith," April said.

"I'm glad you guys made it." Keith put the hot

dogs on a plate and took the bag. "Tell Nick thanks." He set the bag on the bench and asked, "So, how's it going, Mel?"

"I've been better." Melena stole another glance at Dylan.

Keith followed her direction of interest. "Yeah, I'm sure. They got here about a half -hour ago."

"I have to ask." April glowered. "Why'd you invite Melena's bratty sister?"

"I didn't," Keith said.

Kelly set a bottle of ketchup on the table and faced them. "I left a message at your mom's house. Maybe she got it before you did."

Melena glared at her sister and frowned. *Always trying to ruin my life.* She looked back at Kelly. "I'm at my dad's now."

April snatched a corn chip from a plastic bowl on the table and dunked it in salsa. "If Dylan shows up at anything, Cassi is right behind. It's like she has this radar. Poof!" She sprang her hands in the air, almost dropping the chip. "Lucky us, here she is." April cringed and started for the pool mumbling, "You should toss the party-crasher out."

"Not a big fan of your sister, I see," Kelly said with an amused grin.

"Not many people who care about me are," Melena said.

Cassi caught Melena's stare. She leaned up against Dylan's chest and whispered something in his ear. He laughed.

Melena diverted her eyes.

April crossed to where Chad sat on the end of a diving board.

Chad squinted one eye against the sun. "Hey, good looking. I was wondering when you were going to get here."

She squatted and whispered in his ear.

He nodded, then pulled his legs out of the water, picked up his towel, and led her a few feet away from the crowded pool.

Dylan seemed to watch the situation closely.

Kelly talked with little break for air, but Melena didn't hear a word. She was too busy taking in the scene before her.

"You're kidding!" April yelled.

Dylan flinched and glanced back at Melena.

Melena watched him for a moment, then looked back to April and Chad.

"…I mean, who spends money on that? What do you think?" Kelly tapped Melena's arm. "Are you listening to me?"

"Um, I'm sorry, Kelly. I'm having a hard time concentrating with what's going on. It makes me nervous." Melena made an effort to smile.

"You poor thing. Here I am prattling on, not even thinking about what you must be going through. Sorry." Kelly wrapped her arm around Melena's waist and squeezed. "I'm sure it will work out."

Always the optimist. "I really appreciate the company, though."

"You've got it." Kelly smiled.

April hugged Chad. "I'm sorry I can't stay. I'll talk to you later tonight, okay?"

He kissed her lightly on the cheek and smiled. "Sounds good."

April snatched Melena's hand. "Come on. We've

got to go now."

"What happened?"

April glanced over at Cassi and Dylan. "Later. Let's go."

"Okay." Melena turned to Kelly and waved. "I guess we'll see you later. Thanks."

"Sure. Bye."

As they walked through the gate, Melena asked, "Why did you want to leave?"

April shook her head. "Because once I tell you this, I know you're going to freak." They got in the car and April turned to her wide-eyed. "You're never going to believe how ridiculous all of this is. But Chad said that you..." She paused to take a breath. "He said Cassi has a media file with you saying you only went out with Dylan as a joke and that you were just leading him on."

"What?" Melena's head swam. "That's absurd!"

"I know it sounds dumb, but that's what Chad said."

"Has he heard the recording?" She blinked back the tears.

"No." She offered a consoling sideways grin. "But Dylan told him what it said. Chad said it's pretty bad."

I don't understand. This isn't happening. "How is that even possible? I never said that."

"We'll get to the bottom of it." She gave her a hug. "Let's get home and we'll figure it out, okay?"

****

Dylan waited until April and Melena cleared the fence, before climbing out of the pool. He seized his towel off the ground and crossed to his friend. "Chad, what was that about?"

"April wanted to know why you haven't been

talking to Melena." Chad sat on a lawn chair and propped his feet up.

"And you said?"

He shrugged. "The truth. I mentioned the recording and what was on it."

Dylan crossed his arms and squatted to the ground next to him. "And what did she say?"

"She seemed shocked."

"Because she was caught?"

Cassi came up behind Dylan, dripping. "Hey, what are you two doing? The sun is going down soon. You should come back in the pool."

Dylan didn't look at her. "Not now, Cassi."

Cassi huffed and went for her towel a few feet away.

Chad kept his eye on her as he talked, "Dude, why do you even put up with her? She's ridiculous."

Dylan glanced over his shoulder at the pretty brunette. He had no real interest in her. In fact, most of the time, she annoyed him. The problem was he didn't know how to get rid of her without being rude and, in an odd way, she was still a link to Melena. "So, Melena was surprised she'd been caught?"

"I don't know, man. I still say she doesn't seem that cold." He nodded toward Cassi. "Her on the other hand...I don't trust her. My advice, watch your back." Chad swung his legs over the chair, slapped his shoulder, stood, and dove into the deep end of the pool.

Dylan looked over at Cassi. She bent over in her skimpy bikini, probably for his benefit, and met his eyes with a seductive stare. He redirected his gaze. *I've got to cut her loose.*

****

April pulled into the association's lot for visitors and parked in the closest slot. In a daze, Melena pulled herself out of the car and dragged herself to her condo door. "I'm going to go to bed."

"Now?" April looked at her watch. "It's only six o'clock."

"Yeah, well, I'm exhausted and have a huge headache. I'll see you in the morning." She hugged her friend and said, "Thanks, April."

"Of course. What are friends for?"

Melena closed the door to her room and sighed. Without even removing her clothes, she climbed between the sheets and touched her forehead. It was warm. She closed her eyes and tried to relax, but her mind whirled. April's revelation haunted her. *I never said those things, so how could I be on a recording saying them? It must be some sort of trick.* Cassi used to date a tech geek. She even brought home a bunch of technical manuals and videos. Obviously, some manipulative goal to get her man. She was probably capable of making a fake recording.

Melena pouted. *It's no wonder Dylan hates me.* She watched the sun sink behind the hill, and the numbers on her clock flip by the minute. It was two in the morning, when she remembered something concrete. Cassi's strange behavior the morning after Dylan and she had gone to breakfast. *All those bizarre questions. And the recording.*

"That's it!" She sprang from the bed, swung open the door, and rushed into the hallway. "I know what happened!"

She pounded on each door. Slowly they opened, and everyone joined her in the hallway rubbing their eyes and yawning.

"I know what happened," she repeated.

"Calm down," her dad demanded. "What's this all about?"

"I…um…I know why Dylan has been acting the way he has."

"Oh, well, if that's all." Her father walked back to his room. "You can tell me in the morning. I'm going back to sleep." Then he said over his shoulder, "And Melena?"

"Yeah, Dad?"

"Don't wake us up again." He closed the door.

April and Nick motioned for her to follow them into the living room. They sat in a circle on the floor. Melena told them about how Cassi had been acting really strange, about the odd questions, and how Cassi had used the yearbook.

"I was talking about Jason, but on the recording, it probably sounded like I was talking about Dylan. I knew she was acting strange. I don't know why I didn't figure this out weeks ago." She snatched a blanket from the back of the couch and bundled in it. "Now that all this time has gone by, I don't know how I will ever help Dylan see the truth. That I really like him."

Nick held up his hand. "Wait. Okay. So, you're saying Dylan dumped you on account of some stupid recording Cassi made?" Nick scoffed. "That's the dumbest thing I've ever heard."

"You don't believe me." Melena pouted.

"Oh, I believe you. I just can't believe Dylan would fall for it, that's all."

April raised an eyebrow. "Wouldn't you?"

"There has to be some sort of pause or trick in the

recording." He motioned toward Melena. "Besides, she said she'd go to the banquet with Dylan, right? Why would Mel do that, if she didn't like him?"

April nodded.

"Well, then how could he think she didn't like him?"

"Evidence is evidence." April hugged her knees. "How is Melena supposed to get him back now?"

He stood up and crossed his arms. "I'm beginning to wonder if I want her to have him back. He seems a bit brainless to me."

April jumped up and glowered at him. "Of course you don't mean that. If she loves him, she should be with him."

"Please." His voice rose as he stepped forward. "Love can be blind to reality."

"The reality is he's a good guy."

"You don't know that." Nick shook his head. "You've known him how long?"

"I'm a pretty good judge of character."

"Look, I care about Melena and who she's with."

"What, and I don't?"

"You just want to have someone to double date with."

April moved within an inch of Nick's nose, eyes narrowed, lips pursed.

Melena knew that look. She jumped up. "Stop it both of you, please." She pressed between them. "Now *shush*. You're going to wake Dad."

They backed up, but didn't redirect their glare.

"Besides," Melena said, "this is bad enough without the two of you bickering about *my* problem."

April looked at her. "Sorry, Melena."

"Yeah, me too," Nick said.

Melena slumped to the couch. "Cassi has really done it this time, huh?"

"I'm going to wring her neck." Nick seethed. "This time she has really gone too far."

"Well, I guess I'll go back to bed now. Thanks for listening." Melena staggered to her bedroom. She could feel their sympathetic eyes on her back. She shut the door, climbed between the sheets, and listened as their chatter went well into the night.

****

The next day, Melena woke up groggy. She rolled out of bed, shuffled to the kitchen, and turned on the coffee maker. On the counter, a pink sticky note hung off her favorite mug.

Melena,

We decided to go to Del Mar and see if we could find the recording. We're taking Keith and Kelly with us. We should be back by noon. Sorry, we didn't wake you, but we figured you needed the sleep.

Love, Nick.

Melena crumpled the note and tossed it in the trashcan. The coffee perked and dripped into the glass pot. She grabbed the milk and sugar and made herself a cup. As she took a sip, Nick's truck sounded in the driveway. *Uh oh. Keith and Kelly are probably here, too.* She put her cup in the sink and slipped back into her room to change.

"The note's gone, so she must be up. I'll go get her," April said.

April knocked and pushed the door open.

Melena zipped up her jeans and faced her. "Hey."

"You're up?" April smiled.

"It's almost noon. How could you guys let me sleep this late?"

"You needed it."

Melena stepped to the mirror, ran a brush through her hair, then pinched it up with a clip.

April walked behind her. "We've got something you should hear."

They walked into the living room. Nick, Keith, and Kelly hovered around the computer. "Ready?" Nick said.

Melena crossed her legs and folded to the carpet. "Shoot."

Nick clicked the mouse on an audio file. Static filled the air and then Cassi's voice.

"Could you ever fall in love with..."

"Who?"

"You know who?"

"Dylan?"

"She pointed to Jason's picture here," Melena said.

"Are you kidding? No. You know that. I only went out with him because I couldn't bring myself to tell him the truth. Trust me. He's not my type."

"Hmmm? I thought for sure you liked him. I guess that means I can date him if I want to."

"Knock yourself out."

The recording ended. Nick clicked stop and everyone stared at the carpet with gaping mouths. Melena finally broke the silence. "Tell me the truth. Did I sound like I was trying to make a fool out of him?"

They all nodded in a daze.

A swift sense of sadness rushed over her. Melena wiped at her damp eyes. "Where did you find the recording?"

"On her laptop," April said. "She must have edited it and saved it back to her phone."

Melena passed a hand through her hair and sniffed. "Now what?"

"Maybe we could finish the recording and send it back to him," Keith said.

Nick shook his head and touched her shoulder. "Just call him, Melena."

"Why? He's not going to believe me."

"Sure he will," April said.

Melena put out her hand and April helped her up. "Let's go for pizza."

"What?" April shook her head. "Mel, come on."

"Look, I don't want to talk about it anymore. Not about Dylan. Cassi. Or the recording."

Nick stepped forward and touched her arm. "Melena."

"No, I mean it." Her heart hurt, but it was simple. She would talk to Dylan at the banquet. If he hated her, then so be it. She'd move on.

****

Cassi stared at Dylan's number and wondered if she should call him again. No, he was pretty irritated with her. She'd pushed too hard. She always did. But it didn't matter. No matter what, she would drape on his arm at the banquet and watch Melena drool. She thought of her sister and grimaced. *Innocent Melena. Everyone loved her.* Nick, Kevin, Dad. She had a whole crew of friends. Cassi could count her real friends on one hand. Okay, one finger. Beth. Cassi pursed her lips. *But the hag only comes around when she wants something.*

186

Guys were different. Cassi never had to worry about finding a guy. The male species would usually talk to her, but never to her eyes, always to her chest. Maybe that's why she liked Dylan so much. He actually stared her in the eye. Whether he liked her or not, he respected her enough to do that. When Cassi met him at the party, she had approached him in a bikini top and board shorts. She would have moved on to the guys at the volleyball net but was intrigued when Dylan didn't look below her neck. Not the entire night. Well, not that she saw. She pushed out her C chest in the mirror and smiled. *No guy is that resilient.*

But Melena had him. Her sister took the one guy who treated Cassi like a human being and not a Hooters bimbo. Sweet Melena was a woman who could have any friend she wanted. It made Cassi sick. She twisted her hair up on her head and pinched it with a clip. *Well, I'll get even. She isn't going to get him, even if I don't. Though I really want to. He's so hot!*

Cassi tossed the number on the desk, then scraped it back up. Maybe she was playing this all wrong. She grabbed her cell phone and dialed.

"Hi, Dylan. It's Cassi."

He grunted. "I'm glad you called."

"Really?"

"Yeah, about the banquet…"

Oh no. She had to be quick. "Before you say anything, I wanted to apologize."

He was silent.

"I know I've been a bit pushy and kind of annoying."

He snickered.

"I'm sorry. A lot of it has to do with my

187

relationship with Melena." A roar sounded outside. She walked to her window and peered out into the street. A trash truck drove in front of their house and dumped a can in the back. She pushed her window closed and the room fell silent. "We haven't gotten along in years and with all that happened between you and everything..." She willed some tears. "Well, I've been insensitive. Look, I want to be friends."

The line appeared dead.

"Dylan, are you still there?"

He breathed. "Yeah." His voice husky. She pictured him without his shirt, standing over her at the pool.

"I'll pick you up at eight on Saturday."

She smiled. *Yes!* "Okay, see you then." She set the receiver down and did the Cabbage Patch dance across the room. *It's all in the presentation.* She glanced in the mirror. *You go, girl!*

****

With her elbows resting on her chin, Melena sat in the restaurant booth deep in thought. Her friends conversed in an erratic fashion. Nick kept flicking packets of sugar and Keith had told one too many jokes. Kelly prattled on about useless gossip and April was on a mission to order food. Though Melena heard it all, she felt lost in her own world.

"Hey, how about mushrooms?" April asked, folding her gum into a napkin.

"Mushrooms? Gross!" Kelly squashed her face up.

"Okay, fine. What do you guys want?" April looked at Keith and Nick.

Keith groaned and rubbed his stomach. "Anything. I'm starving."

"Melena?" April turned to her.

"Huh?" She snapped her head up. "Oh, whatever. I'm not picky."

"All right, that's it. I'm ordering pepperoni." April swung out of the booth and walked to the counter.

"Do you guys want me to put some music on the jukebox?" Kelly said, pushing out of the high red booth. "They've got some really cool retro-tunes."

"Nah." Keith kissed her cheek. "Let's talk for now."

"But if we can't talk about the taboo couple..." She mouthed, "You know who." Then said, "And we can't talk about the recording. What can we talk about?" Kelly plopped back down on the booth with a pout.

Nick rolled a quarter across the table. "There. See if they have the Stray Cat Strut."

Kelly smiled, snatched the quarter, then swung out of the booth en route to the jukebox.

The waitress walked around her and placed their drinks on the table. "Will you need anything else? Forks or peppers?"

"Nah, we're good." Nick smiled.

The waitress nodded and walked away.

Melena shot Nick a nasty look.

"What? That hurt," he said.

"What's wrong with you? That was rude."

"No, what is wrong with you? Lighten up, will you."

Melena knew she was probably overreacting. She rolled her shoulders back to loosen the tension she felt. If only it were already the banquet and the chance to put this behind her. To try one more time to win Dylan back, and then let go—for good.

Chapter Seventeen

Melena woke up with butterflies in her stomach. D-day had arrived—the summer banquet. She decided to spend the morning relaxing. She planned to take a long bath, then primp the rest of the day. She stepped in the hot bath mixed with scented oil and bubble bath. Laying her head back, she batted at the bubbled surface and tried to relax. The minute she closed her eyes, the Dylan and Cassi situation began to plague her thoughts.

Did he ever really like me? Will he talk to me? How will Cassi react? Do I have the guts to pull this off? Aah! She sat up and hit the side of the tub. *Please give me a moment of rest!* A strand of bubbles adhered to her skin. She swiped them off and sighed. *It's useless. I'm not going to get peace until this night is over.*

Melena stepped out, wrapped her hair in a towel and climbed into a thin cotton robe. When she opened the door, the steam seeped out in waves down the hall. *Nick will kill me if I used all the hot water.* She smiled. *Ha! Retribution is better than a noogie, my dear brother.*

In order to drown out a second more of cognitive torture, Melena decided to blast her music while getting ready. She turned on her stereo and placed a Sanctus Real CD in the slot. The synth sounds blared through her speakers, filling her with adrenaline and an odd sense of excitement.

Melena had just finished blow-drying her hair, when April flew in and turned down the volume. "Seth called. He's in San Diego."

Melena swiveled around from the mirror. "So soon? What happened?"

"He said he wanted to take me to the banquet."

"No." Melena's mouth fell open.

"Yeah." Her voice shook. "I told him I wanted a break and he started crying." April partially covered her mouth. "I've never heard a guy cry before." She melted to the floor with tears of her own. "He told me when I was done experimenting, he wouldn't be there."

"Oh, April. I'm so sorry." Melena squatted next to her and placed a hand on her back.

"Oh, no, don't be sorry." She sniffed and forced a smile. "This is good, right? I need this break and I really like Chad. The tough part is over." She crawled to the bed and snatched a tissue off the end table.

Melena watched her with fascination. Her best friend had forever been resilient. If the same thing had happened to Melena, she would be rubbing off her makeup and crawling into the fetal position. *I wish I could be like her sometimes.*

April blew her nose. Its loud, raspberry sound made her snicker behind the tissue. "Sorry."

Melena giggled. "April, you do know I love you, right?"

"No more than I love you." She hugged her. "Now let's stop all this boohooing. We have a big evening ahead of us."

"I hope you haven't finished with your makeup." She spun April to the mirror. Black goop lined her face, accented by a lovely Rudolf nose and glassy red eyes.

"Wow, I look hot."

Melena laughed and squeezed her shoulders. "Chad won't be able to resist you now."

April turned and rubbed her cheek on Melena's.

Melena shrieked, "No, April."

Her friend backed up, laughing.

"I was almost done with my makeup."

"I thought we could go as twins."

Melena shook her head and retrieved a tissue to wipe the black smudge from her face. "You can go now."

Her friend giggled and walked out the door.

Melena shook her head and finished her makeup. When she was done, she went in the kitchen to grab a bottle of water. Nick was sprawled out on the couch in shorts and a tank top, watching a soccer game.

"Nick. Did you get the boutonnieres?"

"What boutonnieres?" he said, without looking away from the screen.

"You didn't pick them up?" She glanced at the clock on the wall. It was less than an hour before the banquet and she still wasn't ready. "Now we won't have time."

He looked over his shoulder and smirked. "Calm down, I was just playing. They're in the fridge."

She swung playfully at him, but he caught her arm. He glanced down at her sweats. "You're running late, so concentrate on getting ready, okay?"

She eyed his clothes. "Aren't you going, too?"

"I'm ready." He smiled.

"Yeah, right."

"Keith is bringing me a tux any minute. I'm not

like you. I don't need to spend hours in the bathroom doing my hair and makeup."

"How long *do* you plan to spend on your makeup?"

"Funny." He smacked her rear, pushing her toward the room. "Now go get your dress on. Rick will be here in fifteen minutes."

"What?" She glanced at the clock again and shrieked. She ran in her room and yanked the hanger off the rack. Then stopped for a moment to admire the soft material. *I love this dress!* She pulled off the plastic, removed it from the hanger, and unzipped it. She'd just zipped it up, when April walked in.

Melena gasped at the sight of her friend and whistled.

April wore a form-fitting black dress, with long matching gloves and a charcoal pearl necklace. Her short hair was curled and pinned up at the sides with silver barrettes. "You look amazing."

"You too," she said, spinning her to the mirror. Melena's hair hung in soft waves down her back, and the dress hugged her figure, accenting her olive skin.

April pushed against Melena and beamed. "We are going to have the time of our lives tonight."

With a strained smile, Melena worked to hide the angst that just took up residence in her stomach. "Yes, we will."

April blew a bubble through her glossed lips.

"April!" Melena grabbed a tissue and held it under April's chin. "Spit."

She pushed saliva to the front of her mouth.

"I meant your gum."

April laughed. "I know." She pushed her gum into the Kleenex and bared her teeth in the mirror. The doorbell rang and she squealed, "It's time."

"Chad is here," Nick yelled from the other room.

April turned to Melena and motioned down her body. "So, am I ready?"

"As ever."

April hugged her, then walked into the living room.

Melena peeked around the doorway.

Dad and Nick took the time to embarrass April properly with lots of pictures. April glanced over at Melena with a *help me* look.

Melena walked in the living room. "Dad, maybe you should let them get going."

Chad looked her over. "Melena, you look beautiful."

She smiled. "Thanks, Chad. You look good, too." He had on a tux jacket and pants, T-shirt, and tennis shoes. *Totally him.*

Nick raised the camera to Melena and snapped a picture.

She squinted at the flash and covered her face. "Stop, Nick. The moment is captured. Go get ready."

"We'll meet you there," April said, taking that as her cue to exit. "Bye, guys."

Rick arrived a few minutes later. He seemed a bit fidgety, but his smile indicated he was in high spirits. "Melena, you look amazing."

She twirled around and grinned. "Thank you."

Nick shook his hand. "Good to see you, man. You free to surf tomorrow?"

Enrique nodded. "Yeah, sure. Sounds good."

Melena's dad snapped off the TV and joined them in the entryway. "Good to see you again, Enrique. How was your trip this summer?"

"Good."

"Well, you'll have to come by and fill me in, I like to hear missionary stories. It keeps me up-to-date in my work."

"Okay, I'll do that."

Enrique turned to Melena and handed her a clear box. Inside lay a wrist corsage made up of miniature cream roses accented by a gold bow. He withdrew it and placed it over her hand to her wrist.

"Thank you, Rick. It's beautiful." She studied it for a moment, before pinning her white rose to his lapel. Her hands shook as she tried to fasten. Finally, it was set in place. "I guess we're ready to go."

"Not without pictures." Her brother stepped forward and began snapping shots. Melena and Enrique vamped for a few, then started for the door.

"Bye, Dad," Melena said. "See you there, Nick."

They stepped outside and Melena gasped. A white limo was parked in the driveway. "Rick? Why...? What...?" *Please tell me you didn't do this for me.* That guilty feeling perched on her shoulders again.

"My uncle owns a limo company. He said we could borrow it for the night."

"Wow, that's cool." *Thank goodness.* Melena didn't want him to do too much for her. She'd only feel worse than she already did.

The driver opened the door, and Melena climbed in. Her eyes went wide. The inside was plush, with burgundy leather interior, stock bar, TV, and phone. She had seen the inside of a limo in the movies, but never actually ridden in one. She opened the tiny refrigerator. Inside was a green bottle of sparkling apple cider and two crystal glasses.

Rick took the bottle in his hands and unscrewed the cap. "Thought a toast would be in order." He poured both of them a glass and handed one to her.

"What are we toasting?"

"To you making it on your dream volleyball team." He lifted his glass in the air. "I promised we'd celebrate, didn't I?"

"Yes, and I'll drink to that." She clinked her glass against his, then sipped the bubbly drink. She held out her glass for more.

"Not too much now." He grinned as he poured her some more. "You don't want get tipsy."

She laughed. "Funny."

Enrique placed the bottle back in the fridge. His smiled faded slowly, and he stared out the window lost in his thoughts.

Melena peered around the space. He was such a nice guy. *Went to all the trouble and expense to show me a nice time yet I'm using him to get Dylan. Lord, forgive me.* "Rick, I really am sorry about everything."

His eyes met hers. "You've already apologized. Please don't do it again."

"But you did all this…for what?"

"For us to have a good time, and if you'll stop feeling bad, maybe we can do just that." He smiled. "Seriously, don't worry about it. You told me the truth. I didn't do anything I didn't want to do."

Yeah, you're a really nice guy. She half-grinned. *If only my heart could see what my head does.*

The limo arrived at the church gym a little late. People lined the room in almost every open space. Melena scanned the crowd and her eyes stopped at Cassi. She stood alone. Fear clutched Melena's thoughts. *What if he didn't come?* "Rick, I'll be right back." She wove her way through the throng to where her sister leaned against a drinking fountain.

"So, Cassi, did Dylan grow some brains and dump you?"

Her eyes narrowed. "Ha! You'd like that, wouldn't you? But you forget, sis. Guys don't dump me. I dump them." She glanced over her shoulder and smiled. "Don't get excited just because he isn't at my side right now. He's here and still with me. Not you."

"Whatever."

"Great comeback, Mel. Work on that all day?" Cassi sneered and pushed past her.

"Are you ready?" Enrique came alongside her and offered his arm.

The familiar feeling of wanting to bolt jumped in her gut. She pushed it aside. *Not tonight. Big breath in. You can do this.* "Yeah, let's go." She grabbed his elbow, and he escorted her to an empty spot at one of the tables. "Do you want something to drink?"

"Yes, please."

He walked away as Melena studied the room.

The committee had really outdone themselves this year. Silver and black tinsel hung from the ceiling with matching foil balloons and streamers. The tables had black tablecloths with mirrors and floating candles in the middle. A D.J. sat under the scoreboard playing music and, next to him, a horde of hors d'oeuvres and punch decorated a table.

Enrique took a seat and handed her glass of punch with orange sherbet floating on the top.

Dylan flashed in her line of sight. He led Cassi toward an empty chair on the other side of the gym and looked up. His gaze met Melena's, then he looked away with clenched jaws.

An ill feeling washed over her. She couldn't wait. She had to do something. "Rick, I'll be right back."

"Sure."

Melena started for Dylan. Her heart lodged in her throat. She stopped. Then shuffled forward. Then turned back. *I can't do this. This isn't me. I'm the shy girl. The one who sits alone at dances and says what everyone wants her to say.* She looked at him again. He wore a charcoal jacket and a black shirt without a tie. He'd never looked so good. Her stomach hurt. *Why is this so hard? April would be over with him right now. April! Of course.*

Melena caught sight of April and Chad taking their place by Dylan. Melena stared at her until she looked up, then waved her over.

"What's up?" April asked when she reached her.

"I can't do this." A queasy feeling swept over her and, for a moment, Melena thought she might puke. She swallowed. "I can't just walk up to him and talk to him. He's with Cassi, and he's mad at me. I'll make a fool out of myself."

April glanced at Dylan. He was staring at the table, fiddling with a cloth napkin. "Maybe you should try something else to draw him out."

"Like what?"

She grabbed Melena's hand and pulled her toward the stage. "Excuse me," April said to the D.J. "Would you be willing to announce something?"

The guy shrugged. "Sure. Whatcha got?"

April looked back at Melena. "What do you want to say?"

Melena's heart pounded hard in her chest. The room swayed. Her stomach turned. *How am I still standing?* "I don't know, April."

"Come on. This way is painless." She took hold of Melena's forearm. "If you had the nerve to walk over there and say whatever was in your heart, what would you say?"

"What would I say? That he shouldn't believe everything he hears. That I really care about him. That Cassi's a big, fat liar and a sleaze-bucket."

April laughed. "I think the first two will work for now." She turned back to the D.J. "Do you have a paper and pen?"

The guy reached under his turntable and produced a ballpoint pen. Then passed her the back of a flyer. "Here."

April wrote something on the paper and handed it back to him. He nodded and went back to his headphones.

"What did you write?"

"Exactly what you said."

They stepped down, back toward the tables. April moved to return to her seat. Melena caught her arm. "Why are you hanging around Cassi, anyway?"

"I'm not. Chad is hanging out with Dylan. If you'd hurry up and win him back, maybe I can sit with you for the rest of the evening."

April and Melena went back to their dates, awaiting the announcement. The disc jockey definitely tested Melena's patience. He played five other songs before he finally got to hers. The servers had just started serving the salads, when he finally said, "Ladies and gentlemen."

Her heart leapt.

"I have a special announcement this evening from one of our guests. She says, 'you shouldn't always believe what you hear, but know from the night hike to the sea, that everything was real.' This one's for you." Then the D.J. put on a Plus One tune that matched Melena's anxiety.

"I'll be right back," she said to Enrique. Melena rose and glanced toward Dylan's seat. He wasn't there. She walked through the gym searching the melody of faces. *Where is he? Maybe he didn't even hear the announcement.* She held back the tears and went for the door. She had to get outside before she lost it. She reached for the handle. A warm hand covered hers. She looked up and met Dylan's eyes.

"Dylan."

He motioned for her to step outside, but didn't utter a word. As they closed the door, the air became still. *What is he thinking?* She was afraid to ask. Her heart throbbed in her chest. He was close enough she could smell his aftershave. She inhaled and closed her eyes for a moment.

He led her to a wedding gazebo on the back lot. The wind blew against her skin, and she sighed with anticipation.

He cleared his throat and stared at his shoes. "What the D.J. said…is that how you really feel?"

"Yes."

"Then explain the recording, Melena." He looked up and gazed into her eyes. "Everything inside me wants to understand." His features appeared smooth in the amber glow of the streetlight. His jaw was tight, his eyes pleading.

Please voice, don't betray me. "Dylan, you've got to believe me. I have always been honest with you. I've liked you from the moment I first saw you." Her throat tightened. She worked to clear her throat. "Cassi set me up, and I fell into her trap with both feet."

"Set you up?" He stepped forward.

"Remember that morning we went out for breakfast?"

"How could I forget?" He stuffed his hands in his pockets and looked away.

"When I got home, Cassi was overly nice to me. I thought it was odd at the time, but I was trying to believe the best." Melena stood close to him and forced him to look at her. "What you failed to hear in the message was what really happened. I said Dylan out loud, but Cassi shook her head and showed me a picture of a guy from high school." Melena studied Dylan's expression, willing him to understand. To tell her everything was going to be okay. To hold her in his arms once again. "It was a picture of a guy named Jason who I only danced with once to be nice. I wasn't talking about you. You've got to believe me."

"I was so hurt and angry."

"I know. That's why you went out with Cassi."

He stared into her eyes and shook his head. "I was never interested in your sister. She just kind of hung around."

"But you invited her to the banquet."

"No, she asked me to go, but I came here to see you."

Melena gulped. "Really?"

"Really."

She smiled. "I'm so glad." *Everything is okay. He*

doesn't like my sister. Her heart soared.

He started to grin, then turned away, and paced. "I can't believe I fell for that recording. And worse, I never gave you a chance to explain." He faced her and caressed her cheek. "I'm sorry I've wasted so much time." He pulled her to him and brushed his lips against hers.

A surge of electrical current shot through Melena's system. She couldn't hold back the emotion welling inside her any longer. Tears cascaded down her cheeks.

Dylan stepped back and touched her tears with the back of his hand. "What's wrong?"

She wrapped her arms around his neck and smiled. "I'm just happy. I never thought I'd be this close to you again."

"Me, too." He kissed her lightly.

"I thought my sister had really done it this time."

He lifted her chin to meet his gaze. "Let's not talk about Cassi right now, okay?"

She smiled. "Okay."

He brought his lips to hers and, at that moment, nothing else mattered.

Chapter Eighteen

After a few more lingering kisses, Dylan took her hand. He couldn't believe he was here with her. She looked beautiful, even after the tears. "Ready to go back inside as my date?"

She smiled. "I thought you'd never ask."

Suddenly, the realization she already had a date hit him full on. He stopped and looked at her. "Wait. There is one more thing I need cleared up."

She faced him. "What's that?"

He frowned. "The guy you're with."

"Enrique."

He nodded. "Enrique. How does he play into all this?"

Melena sighed. "He's just a friend."

Though the words should be comforting, they pricked Dylan's skin. He let go of her hand and stepped back. "I saw you two kiss."

Melena gasped. "What?"

"Yeah, at *In and Out.*" He crossed his arms, his eyes bore into hers. *Tell me you didn't.*

"You're right. He likes me, Dylan. I won't deny that." She moved close to him. "But when he kissed me, I told him I couldn't be with him. I wanted you."

Dylan searched her expression. A weight dropped off his heart. He slowly took her hand and brought it to his lips. "I'm sorry."

"Don't be." She offered a slight grin. "You have every right to ask. Especially if…" She stopped herself.

"Especially, what?"

She bit her lip. "If I'm going to be your girlfriend."

His heart leapt. He wrapped his arms around her waist and drew her to him. "I like the way that sounds."

She stood on her toes and kissed his nose, then his cheek, and down to his lips. He held the kiss. Her lips soft and inviting. "We'd better go back inside."

She didn't move back, but nodded.

He took her hand, deciding that would be the last time he'd let it go.

****

As soon as they hit the wood floor, Cassi pounced. "Oh, Dylan, there you are." She pawed his arm. "I was looking all over for you."

Dylan, still holding Melena's hand, shoved her off. "Cassi, go away. All you've done is hurt your sister and me. As far as I am concerned, I wish I had never met you."

Cassi stumbled back on her heels, mouth open, eyes wide. "How dare you!"

"No, Cassi, how dare *you!*" Dylan pulled Melena through their friends, toward Melena's table.

Melena glanced across the room to April. She had a smirk that said she obviously enjoyed the moment. Enrique had also seen the exchange. He offered a closed mouth smile as they sat, but Melena saw defeat in his eyes.

"Enrique?" Dylan put out his hand. "I'm Dylan. I think we met at the beach once. You're quite the surfer."

"Thanks."

"I hope you will forgive me for stealing your date."

Enrique shook his head and managed a tight smile. "I knew it was coming. No big deal."

"Can I get you two something to drink?" Dylan stood.

"Um…sure." Melena was glad Dylan was sensitive about the situation.

Enrique nodded and Dylan went to find the punch bowl.

"He seems nice," Enrique said once Dylan was out of earshot. He leaned on the table with his elbows and rested his chin on a closed fist.

"He is." She touched his shoulder. "Rick, I'm sorry this had to happen tonight. I'm sorry if I used you." She searched his eyes. "I really do like him."

"We talked about this already. You don't have to keep apologizing. Really, I'm okay." He slid back in his chair. "How about I go comfort your sister?"

"What? No way." She grabbed his arm. "I wouldn't wish that punishment on anyone."

He laughed, then scooted back in, and placed his napkin in his lap. "Look, if I won't cramp your style, I'll stay for the rest of dinner, then get out of your hair."

"I wouldn't have it any other way." She kissed his cheek.

Dylan arrived with the punch and took a seat next to her. He still took her breath away. His hand rested on the back of her chair, his presence sending shivers along her spine.

April and Chad bounded up and took a seat next to them. "Mind if we join you?"

"Please." Melena smiled. "So, where's my wicked sister?"

"Maybe she found a broom and flew home sulking." Chad winked at Dylan. "Someone was pretty hard on her."

"Like she didn't deserve it," Dylan said.

"Well, she did in my book." April reached for a roll from the bowl in the middle of the table and ripped off a piece. "In my opinion, I think you were too nice."

Melena glanced around the table. Her friends were amazing. "Thank you all for everything."

"Yes, especially me, right?" Dylan cleared his throat, then spoke in a mock feminine voice. "Thank you, Dylan, for making my life miserable. For ignoring me for two months. For dating my sister. Oh yeah, and for not trusting me."

She lifted his hand and kissed it. "Your little speech to Cassi made up for it."

He turned and brushed his lips against hers.

April tossed a crumpled napkin at them and cleared her throat. "Enough you two, or I'm going to lose my appetite."

They pulled away and sat back as the waiters served plates of herb chicken, almond green beans, and twice-cooked potatoes. "This is better than last year's spaghetti." April forked the cheesy-top and smiled at Melena. "Remember when I spilled sauce on my white dress?"

Melena laughed. "You're so good to clothes."

Nick came up behind Melena, squeezed her shoulders, and bent down to her ear. "Saw the show. Everything okay?"

She laid down her fork and turned to hug him. "Yeah, thanks, baby brother."

"It's good to see you smiling again."

She pulled back and grinned. "Nick, you're amazing."

He pulled at his collar. "Yeah, I know."

Playfully, she batted at his head with her napkin. "Nick, this is Dylan. Dylan, my brother, Nick."

"Hey, man," Nick said, putting out his hand. "Nice to finally meet you."

Dylan smiled and shook his hand.

"You want to join us?" Melena waved a hand at the two empty chairs across from her.

He glanced around and shook his head. "Nah, we're at a table with one of Sherry's friends. We may skip out early. Sherry's never been over the Coronado Bridge."

"That's cool."

"I'll meet you back at home, okay?"

"Okay. Bye."

He kissed her cheek and waved to the table.

Dylan held out his fist. "It was nice to meet you, man."

Nick knocked knuckles. "You, too."

Melena watched her brother wrap his arms around his date. Sherry looked gorgeous. She wore a long, burgundy dress and her brown hair was pulled into pin curls. Her green eyes popped with the complimentary color. Melena smiled. Her brother really did look happy. He waved and they exited under the tinsel doorway.

"You and your brother are close, huh?" Dylan said, taking a sip from a water goblet.

She turned back to the table. "Yeah, he's my best friend."

"Amazing how you all have the same mother."

Melena rolled her eyes. "Tell me about it.

Dylan kissed her temple, then cut into his chicken.

Melena stared at him and gulped. Most guys were handsome in a tux, but Dylan wasn't most guys. His model-perfect profile could have appeared on the front of a *GQ* cover. He met her eyes and grinned.

Her cheeks fired up, and she glanced back to her untouched plate of food. Her stomach rumbled. He still had the ability to make her blush, but not to seize her appetite. She picked up her fork and stabbed a green bean.

Everything with Dylan had worked out, so why did she still have an unsettled feeling in her gut? Relief was there, but not peace. Nick was wrong when he said her depression was all about Dylan. It was more about Cassi. Her relationship with her sister was worse than ever. As she thanked the Lord for his help with Dylan, she secretly prayed for a miracle with Cassi.

Dear Lord, help Cassi find you, and let us one day be able to become friends.

April hid her mouth behind her napkin. "Is your brother with Sherry, she's so very, very?"

Melena narrowed her eyes. "Yes, and if you say that again, I'll pop you."

April kinked her head back in surprise. "Sorry, didn't mean to offend you."

Melena shook her head. "Sorry. I just know he really cares about her. She may be my sister-in-law someday. I'm a bit defensive."

"Well, she looks really pretty tonight."

Dylan whispered in Melena's ear, "So do you. Did I tell you that?"

She smiled. "And you're just plain hot."

He raised an eyebrow and moved within an inch of her face. "Shy Melena has left the building. I like it."

She winked and turned to her plate. "I may be sassy, but I can still blush brighter than the rest of them." Even as she said it, she could feel her cheeks warm. *But it was so worth it.*

****

After dinner, Enrique agreed to take a bunch of the stag people with him in the limo, allowing Dylan to drive Melena home. Dylan and Melena followed him out to where the limo was parked.

Dylan shook his hand. "Hey, let's get together and surf sometime. You're pretty good. Maybe you can teach me some stuff."

"Sure. Anytime."

"Thanks, Rick." Melena leaned over and kissed his cheek. "You're a wonderful friend."

"Uh-huh." He nodded. "Always the friend."

She started to apologize.

"No, it's supposed to be this way. See you at practice in a week."

She shook her head. "No you won't. Mr. Co-ed Division B."

Enrique smiled. "Sure, pour salt in my wound."

"Hey, any time."

He waved and disappeared into the limo with a group of girls.

Dylan watched Enrique sit, surrounded by taffeta. "Well, I'm pretty sure he'll be okay."

Melena laughed. "Yeah, I think so."

He faced her and brought one of her hands to his lips. "So, you made the Spikers? Your dream has come true. Congratulations."

"You remembered?"

He lined her jaw with his finger. "Everything you ever said has been like a recording in my head for weeks." Dylan placed his hand on the small of her back and led her to his Jeep. Before opening her door, he placed a light kiss on her cheek. "Doesn't this feel great?"

"What?"

"I don't know about you, but I have spent the past couple of months in a catatonic state. It is so good to finally be with you."

She kissed him. "I concur."

He fastened the top on the Jeep and zipped the windows, then let her get in. "Don't want you to mess up your hair. It's too pretty." He kissed her again, shut her door, and went around to climb in his side. "Do you want to go straight home?" he asked as he put his seat belt on.

No. Not really. "Yeah, I probably should." *I want to spend every moment with you.* "Church is tomorrow." *Please try and talk me out of doing the right thing.*

"Yeah, you're probably right."

And he didn't. She laid her head back against the seat and enjoyed the hour drive back home. He took the scenic Highway One. The moon beamed high in the sky, lighting the ocean below. With a summer full of questions and a new future in the wind, the chatter didn't stop the entire time—a far cry from their first ride home on the bus.

"So, after only one semester, you plan to transfer to UCLA?" Melena twisted, as far as the seat belt would allow, facing him. Her mind reeled. Dylan might actually move up by her.

"For the past painful month," he smiled, "I've spent a lot of time reflecting and writing. I entered a short story in a contest, and I won."

"Dylan, that's awesome."

"It helped me realize my passion. I want to write for a living." The green Brookhurst freeway sign glowed overhead. He pulled off the exit and slowed at the light. "UCLA has an amazing program." He reached over and lightly touched her chin. "Besides, all my friends are up here."

"Not Chad."

"Actually, he's attending Vanguard University in the fall. So, he'll be in this area by next week."

"I didn't know that."

The light turned green. He looked back to the road and turned right.

She shifted in her seat, hoping he couldn't detect the ridiculous grin plastered on her face. "What about your mom and your sister? Didn't you come out here to be with them in the first place?"

His jaw tightened in the amber light. "They're moving again."

"What?" Her stomach flipped. "But they just got here."

"She fell in love with some guy at her work, and he's asked her to marry him."

"But she's only been here two months."

He glanced at her. "I know."

"So, if you don't transfer to UCLA, you'll be moving where exactly?"

"Back to Florida. He's on a research team out there." Dylan gripped the steering wheel and slowed at another red light.

Melena scrunched her eyebrows. "Didn't she just come from Florida?"

He pressed his lips together. "Apparently, she knew Donald from a lab in Jacksonville. They've been friends for years. When she got to San Diego and saw someone she knew, they hit it off. And now, they're getting married."

"You don't sound thrilled."

He sighed. "I want her to be happy, and he seems like a nice guy."

"But?"

"But I don't want her to leave."

Melena lightly touched his thigh. "Are you sure you don't want to go back with them?"

He glanced over at her. A smiled played in his eyes. "Not a chance. I'm happy here." He took a right, turned into her driveway, and killed the engine. "Let's not talk about my mom anymore. Let's talk about us."

The word "us" covered her flesh with goose bumps.

He unhooked his seatbelt and turned sideways in his seat. "Just so we're clear, you liked me the whole time?"

"Yes." She smiled.

"And you never went out with me as a joke, and you're glad to be in my car?" He smirked.

She leaned over and brushed her lips to his. "I think I could fall for you."

Dylan pushed a strand of hair over her ear, then kissed her forehead, her nose, and then her lips. "Yeah, I'm kind of thinking the same thing about you."

She placed her hands on his chest and allowed him

to wrap his arms around her. He pulled her close. Here she felt small, yet safe. His arms encompassed her. *He is so warm, so…* A spicy aroma wafted to her nose, and she took a deep breath. *And smells so good.* She didn't want him to let her go, but she knew they couldn't stay in the car. She looked up at him, and he kissed her again. Everything in her wanted to stay. But there was a reason her father had always trusted her. She made sound decisions that kept her out of trouble. In Dylan's arms, she knew she was weak. She reluctantly pushed back and offered a lazy grin. "Well, I'd better get inside."

He kissed the top of her head, then rubbed her arms. "Yeah, I guess it is pretty late."

She retrieved her purse and reached for the door.

He held up his hand. "No, wait. I'll come around and open your door." He got out, but didn't open her door right away.

She turned around to see his shadow head for the yard. *Where's he going?*

When he returned, he opened her door and handed her a purple daisy. "You guys should think about growing roses."

She smiled and brought the flower to her chest. "The Association maintains the grounds, but I will tell them of your recommendation."

He helped her out and walked her to the door. "Well…"

"Well…" She smiled.

They gaped into each other's eyes. He slowly moved his lips to her mouth. They kissed for a lingering minute and then he moved back.

She slowly opened her eyes. "Wow."

"Yeah, me too." The dopey smile on his face made Melena smile more. "I'll call you tomorrow."

"Church gets out around noon. I'll be home anytime after that." She remembered. "Hey, why don't you come in and meet my dad."

He shrugged. "Yeah, I'd like that."

Melena unlocked the door and walked inside first. She didn't want to find her dad in pajamas. Her dad sat propped up on the tan armchair just inside, watching the news. "Hey, Dad."

He looked up and smiled. "Hi, sweetheart."

"There's someone I'd like you to meet." Melena stepped aside and Dylan peeked around the door."

Her dad stood and put out his hand.

"Dad, this is Dylan. Dylan, my father."

"Barry," her dad said.

Dylan shook his hand and smiled. "Nice to meet you, sir."

"Did you two have fun?" her dad said.

Melena and Dylan exchanged smiles and nodded. "Yeah, it was good, Dad."

Her dad flipped off the TV and motioned to the futon. "Would you like to come in for a while?"

Dylan glanced at his watch and shook his head. "Church is tomorrow, and I have an hour drive back, so..." He looked at Melena. "I should probably get going."

"Well, you're welcome anytime."

"Thank you." Dylan nodded. "Nice to have met you, Barry."

"Night."

Melena took his hand. "I'll walk you out." They went outside and Melena shut the door. "Hey, I still have your hoodie."

"That's right." He tilted his head. "You didn't thrash it with scissors or anything."

"Tempted, but no." She grinned and touched his cheek. "I'm going to miss you."

"So not fair. All that time you were so close, and I blew it." He took a deep breath and sighed. "When will I get to see you again?"

"I know we're living a bit far apart now, so I'll understand if you can't come around every day." She grinned. "I'm free Friday."

"Friday? That's almost a week away."

She grinned. "So it is."

He drew her in and kissed her. "I think that's a bit too long."

"When do you want to see me?"

He looked at his watch and then back to her. "In about ten minutes."

She giggled and pushed away. "Seriously."

He sighed. "Fine. Friday it is. I'll pick you up around six."

"Guess I couldn't twist your arm into moving up here now." She kissed his neck.

"Do that again, and I'll be here tomorrow." He kissed her again and stepped back. "Now, go get some sleep, beautiful girl."

Those words warmed her through. She watched him walk back and start the car, before opening the front door. Even then, she watched until his backlights were mere red pin drops in the distance. She closed the door, leaned against it with a cheesy smile, and sighed. *If this is a dream, give me a tranquilizer drip in my arm. I don't want to wake up.*

Her phone buzzed. She read the text on the screen: *Missing you already. ;)*

"So, things went well," her dad said.

She looked up from the screen with a huge grin. "You could say so." She closed the door. "April home?"

"Not yet." He sat back in his armchair and kicked up the footrest. "Did you have fun?"

"Fun?" She sat on the arm of the chair and laid her head on his shoulder. "Fun just isn't the right word. I had the best time of my life." She faced him. "I got back together with Dylan and he told Cassi off. It was great." Melena leaned back and stared at the ceiling. "I apologized, he apologized, and we made up." She swooned. "We really made up, like nothing had ever stopped us in the first place."

"And what's this about him telling Cassi off? I'm not sure I like that."

"Dylan simply said he didn't appreciate the way she had treated me, and he wished they'd never met."

"Hmm? Well, I'm happy for you, dear. Now, give your old man a kiss good-night."

"Is Nick home?"

"No, but he just called and said they were on their way back."

"Okay. Goodnight." She went to her room and traded her amazing dress for an extra-large T-shirt. A few minutes in the bathroom and she was ready for bed. She snapped off the lights and lay down. A blue glow filled the room, and a soft lull of traffic sounded in the distance. The thought of kissing Dylan played in her head. She closed her eyes, but knew sleeping wasn't an option.

The front door creaked, and then Melena's door opened. "Hey. Can I come in?"

"I'd be mad if you didn't." Melena flipped on the table lamp and sat up.

April climbed next to her on the bed and folded her legs. "Tonight was like the best night ever. What a perfect end to the perfect summer."

Melena snorted. "Hardly perfect."

"No, but the ending was good."

"So, what happened with Chad and you?"

"We stuck around for a few minutes after you took off. Rick came back in to ask you something, but you had left already. Well, I felt sorry for him, so I decided to play matchmaker." A sheepish grin spread across her face. "I tried setting him up with Nancy."

"What?" Melena giggled. Nancy was hardly Rick's type. She was a tall, basketball star with a pinned-back black weave.

"Well, needless to say, Rick was hardly interested."

"No surprise there. Besides, he had a whole limo filled with women. I think he was fine."

April smiled. "Yes, but did you know he took Cassi home, too?"

"What! No way." Melena grabbed April arm. "He took Cassi home? Tell me you're joking."

April pulled her arm back. "Well, I saw them leave together in his limousine. Said they were going to take a ride to the pier before heading back. Who knows?" She swatted at the air. "Anyway, about Chad and me."

"No, wait, April. You can't just tell me something like that and expect to dismiss it so easily."

"Look, he's probably just being a nice guy. It's

Enrique, for goodness sake."

"Yeah, and it's Rick who just got his heart crushed tonight. Rick who is very vulnerable and lonely, easy prey for the likes of Cassandra Harrison."

"Come on, he's a big boy." April leaned against the headboard with crossed arms. "Cassi will not overpower him or anything. He knows better. Just call him in the morning. I'm sure you'll see that nothing happened."

"I hope you're right." Melena lay back and stared at the ceiling. The shadows made all sorts of shapes. She could make out a dog on a leash and what looked like a kid with a balloon.

"Now, about Chad and me," April said, shifting the pillow more underneath her. "We drove to this little park over on Belmont. He brought a packed dessert picnic. Strawberries, whipped cream, and Twinkies."

"Twinkies?" Melena laughed.

April ignored her. "We sat under this huge palm tree. He brought a CD player and read some corny poem." She covered her forehead with her right hand. "It was incredibly romantic."

Melena smiled. "Such the drama queen. Go on."

"Anyway, we talked about dating exclusively. I was a little hesitant after just breaking up with someone else, but I really like Chad. I was just about to say maybe we should wait, when he leaned over and kissed me."

Melena smiled. "And?"

"That, of course, changed my answer."

"Is that all?"

"Is that all?" April mimicked and then tickled her.

Melena laughed. 'Okay, okay. I give up. Sorry."

"Actually, there is more." April giggled. "We had to leave, because a cop came over and shined his flashlight on us. I guess he thought we were a couple making out or something. We assured him we were only talking and promised him we'd go right home." She laughed.

"That's classic."

"I know, right?" April shook her head. "So, all is good with you and Dylan?"

The mention of his name made Melena's stomach flip. "Yes. We talked, we kissed, we agreed to not mention Cassi."

"Smart." April yawned. "Well, I guess you should get some sleep. Church tomorrow."

"I'm going to miss you when you leave." Melena pouted.

"I'm done with high school in January. I'm going to make it my goal to attend college up here in the spring."

"You're not going to walk?"

April shrugged. "Yeah, in June. But I'll be done."

"Cool."

April swung her legs over the side of the bed and hopped up. "Good night."

"Night." Melena flipped the light back off and faced the open window. *What a night.*

"Dear God," she whispered, "thank you for all you've done. Thank you for getting me through this trial. Now, I pray I will be able to patch things up with my sister." She closed her eyes and, before she said amen, she slept.

Chapter Nineteen

Light cut into the dark room and Melena hid under the covers. "Dad, what are you doing in here? What time is it?" She rolled toward the clock and peeked out. *Two a.m.* Her heart skipped. She sat up, squinting at the bright light. "Is something wrong?"

He shuffled forward, his face drawn and pale. "Um, there's been an accident."

"What?" She rubbed her eyes and tried to clear her foggy mind. "What accident?"

He didn't answer.

Her heart pounded in her chest. She leapt out of bed and grabbed her dad's arm. "What's happened?"

"Stay calm, Melena. Your brother is going to need you."

"Why? Why is Nick going to need me? Where is he?" The room seemed to sway underneath her. She blinked to stay conscious. "Where's Nick, Dad?"

April ran into the room. "What's going on?"

"The police called. Nick is at Hoag Hospital. They wouldn't tell me his condition." His voice wavered. "Just that we need to get there." He turned in a daze. "Get ready. I'll call your mom." He turned and left.

Tears flowed, blinding Melena's effort to find anything to wear. She ripped through her drawer and tossed T-shirts all over the floor. "I can't believe this is happening."

"Oh, Mel. I'm so sorry." April stepped forward and hugged the back of her. "Come on, I'll help you find clothes."

Melena wiped at her eyes. "I just need some sweats."

April opened the bottom drawer and pulled out a gray sweat suit and then grabbed a white T-shirt from the pile on the carpet. "Here. Put this on. I'll go get ready and come back in a sec." April walked out.

Melena folded to the ground clutching her clothes to her chest and sobbed. *Please, dear Lord. Be with him.*

****

Melena's heart raced as the three of them stepped through the sliding glass doors of the E.R. The yellow tile and white walls seemed to close in on her. The room, crowded with victims, smelled of bleach and stale air. An overweight woman held a bloodied towel to her shoulder. An old man lay with his head in his wife's lap. A little boy ran back and forth from his mother to the bathroom; a couple, with nervous expressions, stared at a TV in the corner.

Melena's father directed them to a few chairs, then went to question the front desk clerk.

As Melena sat, heat encompassed her chest. She pulled off her jacket and tied it around her waist. The air was thick. She struggled to breathe. "I need to go outside for a minute." Melena stood.

"Are you okay?" April asked. "You don't look so good."

"I'm fine. It's just stuffy in here."

"Go ahead," April said. "I'll get you when we know something."

She stood to go, when she saw Sherry's mother approach Melena's dad. Tears streamed down the woman's face and into the tissue she held at her nose.

"No, I'll be okay. Let's go." Melena crossed to where her dad stood.

Sherry's mom walked away, and her dad glanced at Melena. The grim expression in his eyes confirmed the feeling in the pit of her stomach. The news was bad.

"Sweetheart, why don't you sit down?"

"No, I want to stand. What's happening, Dad?"

He stumbled to one of the orange plastic chairs and sat himself. "Please."

Slowly, Melena lowered herself in the chair next to him. Afraid of what he would say. But also afraid he'd keep it to himself one more second.

"Your brother is in intensive care. It seems…" His voice trembled. He cleared his throat. "A drunk driver hit Nick's car about two hours ago. They were only a few blocks from Sherry's house, when it happened.

Melena gasped.

April clutched her hand.

"Nick is in critical condition." Tears streamed from his eyes. He wiped at them with the back of his hand and visibly inhaled. "And…" He choked. "Sherry is dead."

Chapter Twenty

Melena opened her eyes, her father and a nurse stood over her. She pinched her eyelids closed to clear them. "What happened? Where am I?"

"You fainted. We brought you out of the lobby into an examination room," the nurse said.

Melena sat up. Her heart pounded in her ears. Cringing, she cupped the side of her head.

"Slowly," the nurse said, aiding her. "If you feel better, you can go back into the waiting room, and I'll have someone bring you some juice."

"And aspirin?" Melena grunted.

"Sure." The nurse nodded to her father and left the room.

Melena shifted her legs off the table and slid to a stand. White speckles of light clouded her vision. She reached out. Her dad supported her arm.

"My head really hurts."

"You just fainted. Luckily, April caught your head before it hit the side of the chair."

Melena inhaled deep, and her mind started to clear. Sherry was dead. The woman Nick claimed to love— gone. A tear slipped out, and she sniffed. "How's Nick?"

"He's suffered severe trauma to the front of his head. They said the next two hours would determine a lot."

Her dad supported her as she staggered into the new waiting room reserved for the families of critical patients.

April entered with three coffees. "Hey, girl, you all right?"

Melena nodded, then took her cup, and held it with both hands to her face. The warm steam comforted her. "Can we see him?"

Her dad shook his head. "Not yet. They're prepping him for surgery."

"Surgery?" A guttural noise sounded from somewhere deep in her throat, and she began to cry. Nick meant everything her. She couldn't lose him. *Please God, I beg you. Protect him. Save him.*

The nurse returned with a cup of orange juice and two white pills.

Melena set her coffee down in a free chair and took her bounty. "Thank you."

The nurse nodded and walked away.

Melena threw the pills in her mouth and guzzled down the juice to get the pills to go down her throat. After she swallowed, she switched back to coffee. Her body numb, unable to process all that was happening. The emotional rollercoaster was taking its toll. She tried to focus on the apps on her phone, but the images were a blur. Thoughts of Nick played in her mind. Melena wiped at her eyes and exhaled.

Suddenly, Cassi's voice cut through the silence like the start of a motorcycle at dawn. "His name is Nick Harrison."

Melena grimaced. She turned to April and muttered, "Oh, great. I can't handle her right now."

Her dad rose and walked out of the room.

April wrapped her arm around Melena's shoulder and drew her close. "I'm here for you. Don't worry. I won't let her mess with you."

Melena's mother, Cassi, and Kevin walked into the tiny waiting room. Their father explained the whole situation again. Their mother started sobbing, and Cassi dropped to a chair in a stupor. Kevin didn't seem to know what to do. He started to sit, then stood, and next walked out saying, "I'm going to the bathroom."

Melena glanced over at Cassi. She stared at the floor, her expression blank.

Dear Lord, I know this isn't the time to hold grudges. Please give me the strength to swallow my pride and be there for her. I know I was gloating earlier, but she's hurting now, too. Help me do the right thing. She stood up and took a step forward.

April grabbed her hand and hissed, "Where are you going?"

"To comfort my sister," she whispered back.

She raised an eyebrow and snapped her gum. "Really?"

"Really." Melena knew her voice held more confidence than the rest of her. Inside, she was butter in a frying pan. Melting fast. Adrenaline pumped through her system as she crossed the tiny room. She sat on the edge of the chair next to her sister and took a deep breath. "Cassi?"

She turned her back. "Go away."

Melena peeked over at April. A smirk revealed her concerned amusement.

"Nick is going to be okay. God's in control."

"God?" She wiped at her cheeks. "What a joke! Leave me alone, Melena. I mean it. I don't want you near me."

Of course, Cassi was angry with her. They hadn't exactly had the picture perfect day. *Maybe I need to clear the air first.* "Look, Cassi. I'm sorry about what happened at the banquet."

She glared at her with narrowed eyes. "How *dare* you bring that up right now."

Melena pressed her lips together. She knew this wouldn't be easy, but it was the right thing to do. "Look, I don't want to fight. I just wanted you to know God will take care of Nick." She flipped around and returned to her seat by April.

"Yeah, your God really does things for the Harrison family, doesn't He?" Cassi glowered at Melena. "Dad believes in God and look what it got him—divorced."

Heat flooded Melena's skull. "Maybe if Mom believed in God, they never would have gotten divorced."

The two sisters locked eyes with a defiant stare, both willing the other to cave.

A swift wave of sadness overtook Melena, and she diverted her gaze first. "I just wanted you to know everything is going to be okay." Her weary body fell limp against April's shoulder. She closed her eyes to block out the impossible situation and the pain it brought.

"You tried." April rested her head on Melena's. "You can't do more than that."

They remained there for hours with little conversation, only eating and sleeping to survive. Several of Nick's friends dropped in, including Keith and Kelly. Dylan drove up the next evening. When

Melena saw him, she collapsed into his arms and sobbed against his chest. He held her for a while, stroking her hair, then looked to her dad. "I thought maybe we could spend some time praying together."

Her father nodded. "I think that's the right idea."

Melena glanced at her sister. Cassi toyed with the end of an eraser with her drawing book closed. Her mind probably lost enough to avoid the ego-crushing presence of Dylan.

April slid a chair close to Dylan; Melena and her dad did the same. The four joined hands.

Kevin walked over. "Can I join in, too?"

"Of course." Dylan let go of April's hand and scooted back in the circle.

Kevin straddled the chair and took his hand.

Cassi pivoted away, burying her head in her lap. Their mom left the room.

"Dear Jesus," her dad said, "We place Nick's frail life in your hands. We ask for a miracle." His voice choked with tears.

Dylan cleared his throat and said, "You said, Lord, that when two or more are gathered you will hear our prayer. Please heal Nick. He has so much to offer you."

Tears poured down Melena's cheeks. She wanted to pray, but she struggled to find her voice. *Lord, help him.* She sighed. "Jesus, you know I love my brother. I know his life is in Your hands..." She couldn't continue.

"Mr. Harrison?" came a voice.

Everyone let his or her hands drop.

Melena opened and wiped her eyes, awaiting the news.

Her father rose. "Yes?"

"Your son is awake and he has asked to see you."

The room filled with cries of joy. Cassi jumped up and hugged Kevin.

Melena grabbed April in a hug. Then kissed Dylan. "Thank you, Jesus." She looked at the nurse. "Can we see him?"

"We need to keep it to just one visitor at a time. He's not out of the woods yet, but he has stabilized."

Her mom and dad left with the nurse.

"See, Cassi." Melena folded her hands and held them to her chest. "Prayer works."

Cassi leered. "He's not out of the woods yet. Remember?"

Melena rolled her eyes and looked back to Dylan. "Thanks for being here."

About ten minutes later, her parents appeared in the doorway. Her dad looked at Melena. "Nick wants to see you, sweetheart. He's in the room at the end of the hall on the left."

Melena squeezed Dylan's hand, jumped up, and dashed toward the exit.

"Figures," Cassi said, snatching a magazine from the table in front of her.

Ignoring her, Melena pushed through the double swinging doors and down the hall. She turned the corner into his room and gasped. Nick's usually chiseled features were puffy and bruised. His lips chapped and bleeding. Taped to his left eyebrow was a white dressing and his leg was in a soft cast. Tubes ran from his arms and face. A rhythmic sound of breathing pushed in and out through machines. The pounding of his heartbeat evident by a monitor in the corner.

She licked her lips and inched forward.

His head shifted slightly, and his eyes opened through swollen slits. "Melena?"

Holding back her tears, she rushed forward and laid a hand on his shoulder. "I'm here."

He attempted a smile, then moaned, "Whatever you do, don't make me laugh."

She giggled despite the lump in her throat. "I was so worried."

"Not me. I knew either I'd wake up in heaven, or I'd be okay here. Either way, I'm good."

Melena pulled a chair next his bed and rested her hands on the mattress. "I really love you, you know that?"

"Yeah, the feeling is mutual." He coughed, then groaned, "I'm sore."

"Can't imagine why."

He felt along the bed for her hand.

She slid it into his and searched his eyes. It hurt to see him so broken. Love poured from her chest. The emotion caught in her throat, and she swallowed. *Lord, please be with him. Heal him. I can't lose him.*

"Melena, I need you to be honest with me."

She sat forward. "Of course. Always."

"Mom and Dad wouldn't tell me what happened to Sherry."

There was a sudden jolt to her stomach. Melena diverted her gaze to the corner of his blanket, afraid to reveal the truth. The memory of her brother wrapping his arm proudly around Sherry at the banquet still lingered close. *How can I tell him?* She dreaded meeting his eyes, for fear he would know the truth. *The love of your life is dead.*

He squeezed her hand. "Melena, please. I need to

know."

She resolved herself to face him. A tear fell to the sheets as she lifted her eyes to his. "Sherry, um…" Her voice caught. "I'm so sorry, Nick."

He nodded. His eyes welled with tears. A resonant sob permeated from his chest. His face contorted in grief. *Oh Nick.* Her heart ached for his loss. She clutched his hand and rested her head on his arm.

For a long while, he cried. Then sat in silence, then cried some more. Finally, his crying stilled. "Melena?"

She met his eyes. "Yeah?"

"You know, I always assumed I was indestructible. But I'm not."

She scooted her chair to face him better.

"There are no guarantees."

"I know."

He attempted to sit up, but wrenched in pain.

Melena handed him the control for his bed and fluffed his pillow. "Maybe you should sleep."

"I want you to fix things with Cassi."

She sat back. "I've tried. She isn't hearing me."

"She'll hear you." He stared her in the eye. "Send her in next."

****

In the far corner of the room, Melena's mom waited in quiet hysterics. The woman had shown more emotion in the last week than in Melena's entire life. She wished she could comfort her, but that wasn't going to happen. Her mom wouldn't want it.

Dylan and Keith got up to go get everyone some coffee and snacks. Kevin slid next to Melena and laid his head on her shoulder. "Do you think Nick will be okay?"

She wrapped her arm around him and pulled him close. "I hope so."

Her mom looked up and stared at them with glassy eyes. "Come here, you two."

Melena and Kevin exchanged surprised expressions. They stood in unison and crossed to the empty chairs on each side of her.

She shifted up, wiped at her eyes, then grabbed one of each of their hands. "I wanted to apologize for my behavior lately. With Brian's decision to leave me..." Her voice trembled. "I haven't handled it well."

What could Melena say? That she agreed. That she was hurt. Angry. Bitter. None of those would help and would only hurt. So, she stayed quiet and offered a consoling grin.

"I know I'm not much of a mother. But looking at Nick like that..." Her voice wavered. "I know I love you kids with all my heart. I'm truly sorry for everything."

A sledgehammer smacked into the invisible wall in Melena's heart. Tears coursed down her face, she grasped onto her mother and held her tight.

****

Melena waited for Cassi to return. When she finally did, all hope died with her sullen expression. Her eyes were hard, her mouth set in an incessant pout. She walked past Melena and flopped down on the chair in the corner.

Lord, why is she so angry? Help me to understand her. Help me to reach her. New emotions coursed into Melena's heart. Bitterness turned to sadness. Dislike to compassion. Her sister wasn't a jerk and wasn't evil. Something was wrong.

Melena crossed to Cassi and edged into the chair next to hers. "It's good about Nick, right?"

"If you say so."

"Did you two talk?"

"No, Mel, we played checkers." She flipped her hair and faced the wall.

You never make this easy, do you, Lord? Melena pinched her lips together and inhaled a deep breath through her nose. "Why are you so angry?"

Cassi tilted her head sideways and glared at her. "Who says I'm angry?"

"You'd have to be to do the things you do. To talk the way you talk."

Her eyes tapered to a thin line. "The things I do? Please. You're hardly a saint."

No matter what the cost. "Cassi, come on. I don't lie to my parents, trick guys, or steal my sister's boyfriend." Melena feigned a grin. "Look, I'm trying here. I want to know why you find pleasure in being cruel."

Cassi studied her cuticles with determination, but didn't reply.

The acute silence lay thick between them. At one point, Melena opened her mouth to speak, but clamped it shut. Something in her said to wait. *I can do that.*

Finally, Cassi spoke. Her voice almost inaudible. "You and Nick are so close. You understand Dad and have a relationship with him. Can I help it if I'm jealous?"

"Cassi, I..."

"Let me finish."

"Sorry."

Cassi peered up, her face damp, her eyes red. "I'm

232

in a family with four siblings, and the only place I feel welcome is at Mom's house. Imagine that. I feel normal at Mom's. What does that say about me?"

Melena understood. The only true relationship Cassi had was with a woman who was incapable of intimacy. "I always thought you were more at ease at Mom's, because you and she were so much alike."

"Ha!" Cassi shook her head. "I have no choice. At least if I embrace fashion, then I have her attention. As shallow at it may be, it's all I've got."

"But Dad loves you, Cassi."

She wiped at her face. "He tries, but he doesn't understand me. I'm not religious like you."

"He loves you just the same." Melena carefully touched her shoulder. "That's the cool thing about Christians. We love everybody."

"Yeah, okay." Cassi sneered. "That's why you condemn everybody to hell and stuff your religion down their throats."

"When was the last time you saw Dad on a street corner yelling turn or burn, buddy?"

Cassi rolled her eyes. "You know what I mean."

Melena had had the same battle with many people at school. They said Christians were arrogant and vindictive because they tried to persuade people over to their side of faith. She sighed. If only they understood why—that a Christian believed Jesus was the only way to heaven and the alternative was hell. Therefore, they told people out of love because they cared about their final destination, but Melena didn't believe in hammering it over their heads either.

"Dad loves you, Cassi. He just wants what's best for you." Melena sat forward. "So do I."

"And you think Christianity is best for me?"

"I'll love you no matter what you decide. But yes."

She turned away and stared at the muted TV on the far wall. "I can't do that just yet."

"That's okay. Just know I don't want to fight anymore. I want to be your friend."

"We're sisters. We're supposed to fight." Cassi faced her with a slight grin.

Melena smiled. "Yes, but just because we fight, doesn't mean we have to be enemies."

Cassi stared at her for a while, without a word.

The nurse entered. "Nick would like to see Melena again."

Melena stood and started for the door.

Cassi caught her arm.

Melena faced her, her eyes searching.

"Don't give up on me," Cassi said.

"Not a chance." Melena grabbed her and they hugged tight. Tears welled in her eyes. Oxygen pressed out of her lungs, but she didn't care. Melena didn't want to let go. *Thank you, Lord.*

Epilogue

Melena peered under the volleyball net and eyed the server at the back left corner of the court. The tall African-American woman had stuffed the ball in Melena's face a dozen times already. *Not this time.* Melena tipped forward on her toes and readied herself for game point. The thud of the ball being launched sounded, and she shot into position. Her teammate, Jan, leapt in the air and set the ball to Melena. The ball lifted off her fingertips to the woman to her right. Slam, it went down. The opposing team scrambled to retrieve the ball. Everyone moved, but no one touched it. The ball landed on the floor. It was the Spikers' ball. Two points to win the game.

Melena stepped back to the serving line and glanced over to the bleachers. Dylan and April cheered her on with huge grins. He winked at her, and Melena smiled. *Concentrate. Inhale.* She tossed the ball in the air, and it whizzed over the net. It hit hard in front of the middle person. *Yes!* Melena pumped her fist in the air. The stands went wild.

Match point. One more and the Spikers won the season. All eyes were on her. The room fell silent. Melena tossed the ball in air and smacked it with her palm. It shot over and was retrieved by a bump to the front. Set. Spike. Melena dug under it and popped it to the front. Set. Spike.

The opposing setter tipped it, and the ball flew backward out of control. Three team members scurried off the court to bring it back in play. It hit the floor.

The Spikers jumped almost in unison. The team slammed into each other, hugging, squealing, elated. Melena was in the middle of the congratulatory circle and worked to breathe. She pushed out to see Dylan run from the stands. He snatched Melena into his arms and kissed her. Her heart soared.

"You did it!"

She smothered him in kisses and squeezed him tight. April ran at her and embraced her.

"Can you believe it? We won!" Melena's heart was beating double the normal rate. She couldn't stop smiling. "Let's celebrate."

"Aren't you going out with the team?" April asked.

"Nah, they'll be partying, and I'm in no mood to babysit a bunch of drunks. How about we grab the gang and meet up at my house?"

April frowned. "Are you sure? I don't think Nick is going to want us there."

Nick had practically lived in his pajamas for months, not venturing anywhere other than school and home. He was behind in most of his classes and had shed at least ten pounds. They were all worried about him, but no one knew how to help.

"I know he doesn't, but he needs us there. Sheltering him isn't helping him. It's enabling his destructive behavior." Melena knew she sounded bolder than she felt. Inside, she was afraid he'd be mad, and it would alter their relationship. Though he tolerated Melena, his attitude was far from cordial.

"You're starting to sound like me." April smirked.

"Just let me get my purse."

Dylan wrapped his arm around Melena's waist and pulled her to him. "I've missed you this week. I hate to share you."

She kissed his nose. "I know. But if you're good, I bet Dad will let you stay on the sofa tonight, and we can get breakfast in the morning."

"If I'm good, huh?" He tickled her side.

"Okay, you love birds, let's go," April said.

Melena looked around. "Where's Chad? Didn't he come?"

"He had to take off at one point, but he'll call soon. I'll have him meet us at the house."

As they walked toward the exit, team members stopped to hug her and congratulate her on the final serve.

"Hey, Mel."

Melena knew that voice. She turned around. "Cassi?"

Cassi smiled and held out her arms. Melena filled them. "You came?"

"Wouldn't miss it." She stepped back, and a tall, blonde guy came alongside her. "Mel, this is Kip. Kip, my sister, Melena, and her boyfriend, Dylan."

Dylan shook his hand. "Nice to meet you, man."

Kip nodded.

Melena recognized him as the quarterback at Cassi's school. Melena had gone to watch Cassi cheerlead for a game a few weeks ago, and he was the talk of the night. Supposedly, he had his pick of schools for college.

"Well, I just wanted to say hi." Cassi grinned at her new man, and he returned the smile. "We're on our way out."

"Well, if you get bored, stop by the house. We're having everybody over to celebrate."

Cassi stared down at the wood floor. Her smile lost. "I don't know if that would be a good idea."

"Why not?" Melena asked.

"Just because you and I are okay, doesn't mean your friends want me hanging around." Cassi peeked over Melena's shoulder at April, the one hardest to win over. She firmly believed in "fool me once, shame on me." Melena tried to tell her that wasn't how the saying went, but April said that was her version and she was sticking to it.

"Well, forget them. Just come by and see Nick while you're up here." She squeezed Cassi's hand. "He needs the TLC."

She imparted a tense smile. "Sure, maybe we can do that."

Melena glanced back at Kip. "Nice to meet you, Kip."

"You too, Melena." He smiled, then steered Cassi toward the exit.

"Wow, quite the transformation," Dylan whispered. "I almost didn't recognize her with all those clothes and the lack of snide comments."

Melena elbowed him. "*Shush.*"

He laughed and escorted her back to where April sustained small talk with a child.

"You ready?" Melena said.

April nodded. "Bye, Sarah."

"Bye," the pig-tailed blonde said, before skipping away.

They walked out to the Jeep and piled in. The top

was down. Melena pulled out her hair and let it fly as they started down the road to home. Her excitement hard to contain. A fantasy end to her longtime dream.

****

When they arrived at the condo, all of their friends were waiting outside. "Boy, news travels fast," Melena said, unlocking the door.

Keith and Kelly snagged a seat on the couch, smiling constantly. More than usual. Hard to believe that was possible, considering Kelly's usual cheery disposition. It was almost toxic. Melena knew why though. Keith had asked Kelly to marry him only a few days ago. She, of course, said yes, and now, they were sickeningly happy.

Shawn and Tiffany folded to the ground in front of a laptop. April sat in the chair and Dylan followed Melena into the kitchen. Once they'd cleared everyone's line of sight, he pulled her into an embrace and kissed her.

Her heart fluttered. He still captured her breath with every touch. A spicy cologne heightened her senses. She pulled back and smiled. "Yes, sir. I missed you, too." A bag of tortilla chips lay on the table. "How about dumping those in a bowl?"

"Anything to avoid kissing me, huh?" He winked.

"Actually, the contrary. If we don't keep busy, we won't be leaving this room."

He smiled, then grazed her lips with his. "Fine, where are the bowls?"

"The last cabinet on your left."

He set out for the bowl, and she grabbed sodas and salsa.

"Sspp…" Melena heard a sound behind her. She

glanced around, then over her shoulder. Nick peeked out the crack in the doorway. "Come here, Mel."

She swallowed. *Here we go.* "Be right back, Dylan. Can you take this in?"

He caught sight of Nick. "Yeah."

Melena walked to her brother's room, and he shut the door behind her. "What's everyone doing here?"

"Nick, you need to get out." She stepped toward him and touched his arm. "Start socializing again."

"Why?" He flinched. "I'm fine, Mel. Stop mothering and telling me what to do. Just because I want peace and quiet…"

"No, you want isolation. I know you're hurting, but this isn't healthy."

Nick crossed his arms and fell to the bed, angry. "Get them out of here, Mel."

"Keith's here."

His face remained stoic.

"Come on, Nick." She sat down next to him. "It's been three months since you've talked to anyone besides me."

His eyes narrowed. "So, this is an intervention?"

She shook her head and forced a grin. "No, this is a celebration. My team won."

"Congratulations." He might as well have said, "who cares," because his sardonic tone spoke volumes.

"I love you too much to leave." She kissed his cheek and walked out the door. Her heart hung heavy. She was worried about Nick. His physical wounds had healed, and with the exception of a small scar at his temple, no one would know he'd been hurt. But his loss was greater than his injuries. *Lord, please give him peace again.*

Melena stepped into the living room and spotted Cassi. She shifted from one foot to the other in the entryway, appearing slightly uncomfortable. Her eyes met Melena's with relief. "Is Nick awake?"

Melena waved her over. "He's up, but cranky. You want to risk it?"

Cassi smiled. "Remember, I can be the queen of nasty if I need to be. He'll see me."

"Good luck."

****

Cassi felt more at ease walking into the lion's den, than to stay one more minute with Melena's friends. They had every right to hate her, but it didn't make it any easier. For months, Melena had tried to bring her around them, but to no avail. They either gave her dirty looks or pretended she wasn't present. Melena really wanted them to accept her, and for that, Cassi tried to be civil. But it didn't work. Now she was here for Nick. No other reason. He'd done so much for her, and when he almost died, she promised to make it up to him.

Cassi pushed the door open and pushed out her lower lip.

Nick sat on the floor against his bed with his knees up and his hands cupped over his ears.

Oh Nick. Her heart ached for him. He was such a good guy who didn't deserve this pain. If anyone did, she did. But not him. "Hi," she said, closing the door behind her.

He glanced up and scowled. "It is an intervention. I'm not interested so you can go."

Cassi knelt next to him and dropped her purse on the carpet. "Listen, you're not getting rid of me. You saved me when I needed it most, and now, I'm going to do the same for you."

He dropped his head between his knees, making it impossible for her to see his face. She didn't care; she knew what she needed to say. "When I came to see you in the hospital, you told me that if I didn't get my act together, I was going to live a pretty sad life. You told me there were no guarantees and that if I died tomorrow, where would I go and what kind of life would I be remembered for?" She slid beside him, resting her back against the bed. "You told me you loved me and wanted me to be happy."

She rested her hand on his back. "I love you, Nick, and now I want you to be happy."

His shoulders began to shake.

He fell against her and sobbed. She stroked his hair, sad to see her big brother so broken. She allowed him to cry, without another word. She hadn't prayed since elementary school, but tonight, she'd make an exception. *God, can you help him?*

For a long while, he just lay there. She started to wonder if he'd fallen asleep. His shoulders started to shake again. She lifted his chin. He was laughing.

Cassi wrinkled her eyebrows. "Why are you laughing?"

"When did Cassandra Harrison become the shoulder to cry on?"

"Hey." She pouted and playfully hit him.

He touched her cheek. "I'm kidding." He wiped his eyes with the back of his sleeve. "I'm really tired of feeling this way. It just aches all the time."

"I know, but it will get better if you get your mind off the pain." She stood and held out her hand. "A whole room full of your closest friends are here for you."

He stared at her hand with flared nostrils. "I don't know."

"It's a start, Nick." She stared him in the eye. "You know it's what Sherry would want."

Slowly, he took hold of her hand. He pulled up, stood, then rolled his shoulders back, and exhaled out loud. "Thank you, Cassi."

"Us Harrisons need to stick together." He hugged her close and they walked out hand in hand.

****

Everyone was teasing April, when Nick and Cassi stepped out the door. The room fell silent and everyone faced them. An uncomfortable silence blanketed the air.

Keith took his cue. He let go of Kelly's hand and leapt over the coffee table with hand extended. "Nick, man, how you been buddy? I've missed you." He hugged him with a slap to the back. "You want to go surfing in the morning? High tide."

"Yeah, maybe." Nick glanced around the room. The faces were surely depressing. "I thought you were having a party."

Melena exhaled with the room. "Pizza? Ice cream? Let's eat!" She grabbed Cassi in a hug. "The Spikers won!"

Cassi smiled.

The room erupted in cheers. Melena met both Nick and Cassi's gaze and willed back the tears of joy. For the first time in years, she felt like her family was going to be okay.

A word about the author...

Kimberlee works full-time as an adjunct professor and the Director of Instruction at San Diego Christian College, a cover designer for The Wild Rose Press, and a Creative Arts pastor for San Diego Hope Church.

She resides with her husband and two teenage boys, in San Diego, CA. She has her BA in Human Development, her MA in Humanities, and is currently working on her Ph.D. in Leadership Studies in Education.